# A ROYAL TEMPTATION

## CINDY REDDING

*For My beautiful daughters, Heather and Jennifer.*
*I love you.*

# PROLOGUE

April—Greenwich, Connecticut

Sarina Moore stopped her ancient Volvo at the gates of the Williamsons' sprawling waterfront mansion. At the red-brick guardhouse, she handed her driver's license to the uniformed security officer. "I have an appointment with Mrs. Williamson." Her eyes widened when she noticed the very intimidating gun on his waist.

He scrutinized her license and looked at her, then picked up the phone and spoke into it. Turning back to Sarina, he said, "Follow the road around to the delivery entrance. You can park there. Someone will be waiting to take you to Mrs. Williamson." He handed her back her driver's license, and the security barrier lifted.

Sarina followed the winding drive to the service entrance of the Tudor-style mansion. A young woman in a gray-and-white maid's uniform met her at the door. "Miss Moore, please follow me. Madam will receive you in the downstairs study." Sarina walked across the wood floor down a corridor past the kitchen to the interior of the house.

These rooms were so different from the delivery

entrance. They were big and airy with polished cherrywood floors. The maid knocked on an ornately carved wooden door and waited for permission to enter. She opened the door and stepped into the room. "Miss Moore, ma'am."

"Show her in, then you may go back to your duties."

The young woman turned to Sarina. "Miss Moore, please do enter."

Sarina took a breath and slipped her thumb under the strap of her black faux-leather purse to adjust it on her shoulder. She wore a designer navy-blue blazer with a matching skirt she'd bought at a secondhand store. Sarina squared her shoulders and walked into the study.

The lavish room housed elaborately carved floor-to-ceiling bookshelves on both side walls. An antique mahogany desk stood in front of a picture window that was designed to bring the outdoors in. A Persian rug in warm colors of burgundy and olive covered part of the cherrywood floor. An upholstered Queen Anne sofa faced the center of the room and beside it, a matching wing chair.

"I'm Joanna Williamson." The woman who greeted Sarina sat on the sofa. She was fashionably thin with her blond hair styled into a blunt-cut bob. She oozed sophistication in a berry-colored Chanel suit, and on her feet were black pumps. Gold earrings hung from her ears. A thick gold bracelet was on her left wrist and a gold wristwatch on her right wrist. On her left hand was one enormous diamond ring and on her right hand a square stone sapphire ring.

Sarina walked toward her. "Hello, Mrs. Williamson."

Mrs. Williamson extended her hand toward the wing chair near the sofa. "Please do sit. Would you care for a beverage?"

"No, thank you, ma'am." Sarina perched on the edge of the wing chair, crossing her ankles, and rested her purse on her lap. She was pleased that she wore her only better-quality suit to the interview. Sarina forced herself not to fidget.

"I've read your resume, and I must say I find it quite unusual that you'd be interested in the position of escort."

Her heart fluttered. "Mrs. Williamson, I have the summer off from my teaching position, and I'd be happy to escort you on your Mediterranean cruise."

"Yes, we'll be summering on our yacht, the *Carmella*. My husband, grandson, nephew, along with another escort and I will be on board. We're celebrating my grandson's graduation from law school. I want the whole girlfriend experience. Have you ever been to Europe, Miss Moore?"

"Oh, no, Mrs. Williamson, I've never been further than New York City. I'll do my research on the different ports of call... so that—" Sarina leaned forward. "I hope that's not a problem."

"Do you have a valid passport?"

Her eyes lit. "Yes, I do have one." She smiled.

"Tell me why you feel qualified for this position?"

"I'm a quick study and more than happy to do whatever you wish. I have the time off, and to be quite honest, I need the money that you're offering. It's four times what I make in a year as a kindergarten teacher."

"As long as you're aware of what the position entails and that discretion is of the utmost importance to me and my family's reputation. Would you mind going for a blood test?"

Sarina frowned. *That's odd... but then I had to go for a physical and fingerprints as part of the requirements for my teaching position.* "No, I wouldn't mind. I understand that you can never be too careful. Your offer is quite generous, and Mrs. Williamson, I can certainly be discreet."

"Is red your natural hair color?"

"Yes, it is."

"Very striking with your emerald-green eyes. I'll be in

contact with you after I receive the results of the labs. If all is well, I'll send you a first-class airline ticket so that once school lets out, you can join us on the *Carmella* in San Destino."

Sarina's excitement bubbled into her voice. "Thank you so much for this opportunity. I know you won't be disappointed in me."

Mrs. Williamson handed Sarina a slip of paper with the name and address of the medical lab. "They'll be expecting your call tomorrow."

"Yes, ma'am. Thank you so much."

Mrs. Williamson lifted the receiver on the phone and spoke. "Miss Moore is ready to leave." Before she placed the phone back on the cradle, a knock sounded on the door, and the same maid who brought her here led her back to her car.

Sarina was elated. This money would help her pay some of the tuition for her sister Julia's first year of medical school. The icing on the cake was that she would have the experience of a Mediterranean cruise and traveling around Europe. A dream come true.

# CHAPTER 1

Docked in the Mediterranean by the island nation of San Destino, the luxury yacht *Carmella* swayed in the warm June breeze. Most of her interior and exterior lights were lit. Colorful welcome flags and pennants had been strung above the gleaming deck, waiting for an evening of merriment.

Sarina took a deep breath to give herself courage. When she found the door of the cabin she'd been shoved into unlocked, she knew that quick action was needed. Making her way from the crew quarters, sneaking up the narrow stairs three flights to the main deck. All she could take with her were the clothes she had on.

Mrs. Joanna Williamson, socialite and grandmother, had become her captor. "We discussed the girlfriend experience, and you said you were more than happy to do whatever we wished."

"I didn't know it would involve sex. And that is out of the question."

"I don't have time for this right now." She snapped her fingers, and a security guard came forward. "Take Miss

Moore to a comfortable cabin where she can wait while I make arrangements to send her home. Keep her suitcase and purse with you for safekeeping."

"Yes, ma'am."

Now, while the crew was busy with preparations for the arrival of a special guest, Sarina tiptoed along the hallway as noiselessly as possible, trying to be invisible. Holding her breath as she passed the salon, she was unable to stop herself from peering into the dining room. The room was empty. The table set with fine china; the crystal stemware caught the light from the Waterford crystal chandelier.

She swallowed past the lump of fear in her throat and strode down the gangway. Her heart pounded, almost drowning out the sound of the upbeat music playing through the loudspeakers dotted along the dock. Sarina walked off the *Carmella*. Since her arrival on board this morning, she had been a virtual prisoner in a small, cramped cabin the security guard had brought her to.

San Destino's Grand Marina was a busy place in the summer months, a playground for the rich and famous. Men in tuxedos and women in beautiful evening gowns strolled by. Sarina came to the end of the pier and walked along the dock past the limousines with uniformed drivers waiting for their wealthy passengers, walking on past the Rolls Royces, Lamborghinis, Bentleys, and an array of other expensive cars parked along the dock. With every step she took, Sarina expected to hear one of her captors send out an alarm. It was only pure luck on her part that got her this far.

The music reminded her she was still too close to danger and needed to get farther away from the yacht and the center of town. The moment Mrs. Williamson had told the guard to take her suitcase and purse for safekeeping, she knew that the woman wouldn't send her home all too soon.

Sarina walked along the cobblestone streets, past expensive shops and restaurants. Soon, there were no more street-lights. Keeping close to the side of the road, she made her way onto the shoulder, walking up the steep hill in the dirt around low bushes and trees.

While Sarina was escaping from the *Carmella* and the Williamson family…

~

FILIPPO DROVE his red Ferrari toward the crowded Grand Marina. As he approached the entrance to the dock, the harbormaster waved to him, opened the security gate, and cleared a path, allowing Filippo to drive his sports car right up beside the *Carmella*. Filippo stepped out of the car onto the concrete of the pier.

He was tall with broad shoulders and elegantly dressed in a custom-made tuxedo, his inky black hair cut short. He walked with an air of command as he boarded the luxury yacht.

Howard Williamson, dressed in a tuxedo, and his wife Joanna, wearing a black beaded designer gown, waited on the main deck to greet him as he came up the gangway. The two men shook hands.

Joanna stepped forward, kissing Filippo on both cheeks. "It's always good to see you," she said as she linked arms with him and walked to the salon. "Chad and Derrick are waiting for us."

Both men wore tuxedos. Filippo shook their hands. "Congratulations on your degree, Chad."

"Thank you, I'm happy to have that part over and looking forward to this break before I take the New York State Bar exam."

Howard brought Filippo a drink. "I made you the usual," he said, handing him the glass.

"Thank you. How long will you be in San Destino?" Filippo asked.

Joanna came over. "Not long. We leave for Monaco in the morning. The last two female crew members arrived earlier today. We want to be on our way as soon as possible."

Filippo knew that female crew was code for paid escorts. Chad and Derrick always traveled with the most beautiful women.

A uniformed server walked around the salon, offering an assortment of canapés to the intimate gathering. Another carried a silver tray with crystal flutes filled with chilled champagne.

Joanna said, "Dinner will be served shortly. We've been looking forward to this evening visiting with you."

"I'm thrilled to receive your invitation and arranged my schedule to be back in San Destino."

Filippo enjoyed Joanna and Howard's company and was pleased that they had made San Destino their first stop on their Mediterranean cruise.

Joanna linked her arm through Filippo's, and they led the way into the dining room. Once everyone was seated at the table, Joanna inclined her head, and the servers placed the first course of seafood bouillabaisse before the guests. They chatted and caught up on what had been going on in their lives.

"I had meetings in London and Paris. Late this afternoon, I arrived back from Paris so I wouldn't miss seeing all of you."

Before dessert could be served, a uniformed steward came over to Joanna. He bent to whisper near her ear. Joanna nodded, and the officer turned to go. "Chad, Derrick, I fear you won't have time for dessert. You're needed on deck. Miss Moore is missing."

Chad shoved his chair back with such force, it tipped

over. A steward immediately stepped forward to right it. "Filippo, I apologize, but Derrick and I must say good night now."

"It's understandable. Please go about your business." Then Chad and Derrick hurried from the dining room.

Howard turned to Joanna. "What's the problem, darling?"

"Oh, nothing the boys can't handle. It won't interfere with our departure tomorrow morning." He nodded.

"Filippo, we have a new Italian pastry chef, and I asked him to make you one of his specialties."

The dessert was served, and then Howard said, "Filippo, would you care for an after-dinner brandy? We can sit up on deck."

Filippo stood and took Joanna's hand. He bent over it and kissed her hand. "It's always a pleasure to see you. Thank you for a lovely evening."

"I hope we see you again over the course of the summer."

He and Howard walked up to the top deck. Howard brought out a cigar box. They both lit a hand-rolled cigar.

"I read your report, and then I toured the hospital construction site last week. I'm impressed with the progress."

Howard dragged on his cigar and then said, "We may get this in ahead of schedule and under budget."

"I've always had confidence in your abilities. That's why I recommended you to the board." Filippo glanced at his wristwatch. "It's getting late, and I have to get going. Have a good trip." The two men shook hands, and then Filippo left.

SARINA RESTED FOR A MOMENT. She'd been walking for the past three or four hours. The road had narrowed several miles back. She glanced down at her cream-colored slacks smudged with dirt. Her salmon-colored blouse clung to her body, and her wedge-heeled sandals hurt her feet. She'd worn the same outfit for two days now—ever since she left the US.

On the side of the narrow, winding road, Sarina removed her hair clip, then ran her fingers through the strands of hair hanging past her shoulders. She twisted the length, securing the thick curls on top of her head with her clip.

The road was quiet. Not one car had gone by for some time. She needed to stop to rest for more than a moment. There were a few houses in the distance, but she couldn't bring herself to knock on someone's door at this time of night.

It was very dark now, and she was unable to see much, although the night air was filled with the perfume of gardenia and lavender. It all must look beautiful during the day. At this time of the evening, there was only the yellow glow from the interior lights of homes that sporadically dotted the hillside.

The moon was making its way across the night sky when the sound of a car approaching stopped her. She slipped into an area dense with palm trees. From there, she could see the headlights of the car as they lit the road. It was too dark to see the car or even the driver from where she hid.

Her heart pounded. She hoped it wasn't Chad or Derrick. By now, the Williamsons must know she'd escaped their clutches. Sarina remained by the trunk of a palm tree until she could no longer see the red taillights of the car. The moonlight dappled the area, so she tried to stay in the shadows as much as possible. *What am I going to do? I have no money, no clothing—nothing. How naïve of me to believe that I could get such a high-paying summer job. I should have known that I would have to sleep with someone. Escort,* she huffed to herself. *Really? The money they'd offered blinded me.*

A car pulled off the road close to where she walked. She crouched down by a palm tree.

"It had to be her. Go around and shine the headlights on that area over there."

A chill went up her spine. Unable to see the two talking, she dared not move or breathe as terror consumed her. She pressed her body against a palm tree, ignoring the bark digging into her skin. Drawing in a slow, deep breath, fearful of moving, waiting, praying they would go off in the other direction.

"No, it may have been an animal you saw. It wasn't the redhead." The car engine turned on, breaking the silence.

Sarina watched as they drove away, grateful they didn't find her. She waited for what seemed like an eternity before she rose from her position on the side of the road. *Animals. What kind?* She shivered as a chill crept up her spine. She stepped out of the bushes, onto the road, deciding it would be safer to walk on the road. If a car drove by, then she would go back into hiding. She'd been walking for an hour without seeing another car. She stopped and looked around. The full moon cast a silver light on the glade beside the road.

She glanced up in the distance and bathed in moonlight high up on the mountain stood a massive castle. *Home to the royal family of San Destino.* Exterior lights framed the stone structure.

The sound of a car speeding up the road broke into the silence. Sarina dashed for the grove of palm trees on the side of the road, stepped on a stone, and twisted her ankle.

"Damn!" Sarina cried, landing in the middle of the road, flat on her stomach, the breath knocked out of her. She scrambled to get up as the car skidded around her and came to a screeching stop a few feet from where she lay.

"Don't get up. Are you hurt, in pain?" A man crouched down beside her. *Thank God it isn't Chad or Derrick.*

"Let me help you." He reached for her arm. "Let's make sure you didn't break anything." His voice soothed her.

She sucked in air. "Ooh, I think I'm okay." With his help, Sarina pushed herself to a sitting position.

He continued to hold her upper arm. "Can you stand?"

The palms of her hands stung. She shoved her hair out of her face. "How fast were you going? You could have run me over."

"Then you should be grateful I have quick reflexes."

She heard the hint of humor in his voice. Sarina jerked her head up in his direction, ready to tell him a thing or two about his reflexes. The words died in her throat. Silver beams of moonlight shone on him, and she could see he was handsome. The drop-dead gorgeous type. His black hair was cut short, a lock falling over his forehead. His brows were perfect, his nose straight, his high cheekbones chiseled onto his face and his lips… sculpted, beautiful, bow lips.

While he crouched down by her side, he pulled on his bow tie. It hung open, and in the same move, he opened the top button of his white shirt.

"Well, don't just stand there with your quick reflexes. Help me up." She put out both her hands.

A smile spread across his full bow lips, and he held her hands. His were warm, and his long-tapered fingers closed over hers. He pulled her up.

"Ouch!" Pain radiated through her ankle.

"You're hurt. Allow me to help you." He bent and scooped her into his powerful arms.

Instinctively, her hands moved to the wide expanse of his shoulders, clutching the fabric of his tuxedo. His sexy, clean scent reached her nostrils.

"I'm going to help you sit in my car, then I can determine how badly you're hurt." He walked toward his car. "Whatever are you doing out here alone? There aren't too many people that come this far up the road."

"Oh no, I hear another car. Please, help me." She whimpered.

His deep baritone voice penetrated her fear, soothing her. "I promise I won't hurt you, and I won't let anyone see you. It will be all right." He moved toward his car, and she tightened her arms around his neck, hiding her face against his chest. His spicy scent filled her head.

He whispered, "Let me turn off the headlights, and then we'll go behind this tree. Will that be okay?"

She nodded.

Sarina gazed up at the man who held her snug in his powerful arms. Her eyes drifted to his lips. What would they feel like against hers? Her lips parted.

He lowered his head. "I know I'm a stranger, but don't be scared. Once that car passes here, it will eventually need to turn around. This is a private road."

She relaxed into the softness of his gentle words. Her heart slowed, no longer pounding in fear. "Okay, I'll try not to. You make me feel safe," she said. Their lips were so close, Sarina groaned and couldn't pull away. His sensuous lips touched hers. Sarina turned into him, melting in his embrace, and he slid his firm lips over her mouth.

She wasn't lying. She felt safe in his arms. Her fingers pushed into the short, thick hair at his nape. His tongue slipped into her mouth, warm and hot, twining with hers. He tasted of brandy and cigars; he tasted as good as he smelled. Her nipples tightened, and she pressed her breasts into his chest as pleasure seeped into her body. The place between her legs burned. Her sluggish brain spun, and she pressed her open palm against the wall of his chest, pushing him away. *What am I doing?*

"Shh, listen, I told you they're coming back down the

road." Once more, his lips covered hers. The car passed by and then sped away.

She dragged her lips from his. "Put me down this instant," Sarina said with a voice that was strong and determined, her schoolteacher voice. "Put me down."

He carried her to the passenger side of his car. The rooftop was down. He opened the door and then placed her on the leather bucket seat. "There you can rest until we determine how badly you hurt yourself." He spoke as if nothing had happened, as if he'd never kissed her.

Her lips throbbed from his mouth. She could still feel the pressure of them against hers. Her reaction to his kiss mortified her. *Thank God he's not gloating.* Sarina tried to get up.

His voice thundered. "I said sit and don't move. You may cause more damage."

"You did quite enough damage, the way you were speeding." *And that kiss, I want more. I must be losing my mind.*

He chuckled. "This is Europe. We all drive fast. Where were you going? Do you have family here?"

"No, I don't have anyone here. I know it must look odd, me walking alone at this time of night. But I... was... lost." The half lie tasted bitter on her tongue, but the truth would be worse. After all, she didn't know who he was. What would she say? *I was running away from*—what—*a situation of my own making?*

"I should take you to the hospital. They can X-ray your ankle—"

"Oh no, please don't do that. Just leave me here. I don't need you to drive me anywhere. I can take care of myself."

His deep voice was firm. "I won't leave you here alone. Tell me where I may drop you."

"I can manage quite well by myself."

"Are you sure about that? I find you sprawled face down in the middle of a private road—"

"You're the reason I fell—"

"We won't argue the point. Just know I'm not leaving you alone in this unpopulated area. You may as well resign yourself to that fact. Tell me where you want to go."

She needed a moment to think of what to do. She had to find a job so that she could get back home. The breeze from the sea brought a chill to the night air. Sarina sighed and frowned up at him. "Don't you have anything better to do? I told you I'm fine. Let me out of your car, and you can be on your way."

~

HE GRITTED HIS TEETH, something he never did. He was tempted to go, although he knew he couldn't leave her alone at night by the side of the road. He shrugged a shoulder.

"Please leave me be. Let me get out of this car, and then you may go."

His eyebrows shot up. His thoughts exploded. She'd dismissed him? *This curvaceous nymph of a girl is telling me to go? Incredible! Absolutely unbelievable!* He grinned. *She doesn't know who I am.*

The moonlight streaming down where she sat gave him a better view of her. Strands of long hair fell in waves, framing her oval face and falling over her shoulders. He could see the tresses curling around her breasts.

She had a mouth made for kissing with a full lower lip. His groin heated and throbbed. He wanted to suck her lip into his mouth again. *She is beautiful... But when she speaks, it's all acid.*

"No, I think you're finished giving orders. I know I'm a stranger, and you don't know anything about me, but I promise I won't hurt you..."

The way she looked bathed in moonlight reminded him

of an angel. Every single one of the little pearl buttons on her blouse was buttoned, all prim and proper. She tried to get up, but he wouldn't allow it. His voice, full of authority, thundered, "Sit and don't move." Then he lowered his voice. "If you knew me, then you would know that on San Destino, I'm the one person you can trust the most." He crouched down on his haunches and looked into her eyes. "Will you tell me where you were going?"

He watched as her shoulders drooped.

She said in a soft voice, "I actually don't have any place that I was going. I'll be seeking employment, and had it not gotten so late, I would keep walking in this direction," she pointed farther up the road, "to see if there may be a hotel or possibly a business district that might need some extra summer help. There's also the palace up ahead. I was going to see if they needed any help. If that didn't work, I would walk to the town and find some sort of job."

"Oh really, you were going to the palace, just ask the guards to let you pass, *tap, tap* on the door, and ask if, what? They could use you in what capacity?" He wiggled his brows. "Upstairs maid?"

Shaking her head, her eyes downcast with her hands folded in her lap, she looked devastated.

He decided to take matters into his own hands. "Let me introduce myself."

She looked up at him.

"My name is Jason Donato." A name he hadn't used in years rolled off his tongue. He gave a slight bow.

"I'm Sarina Moore."

Jason closed her door, walked to the driver's side, and slid behind the steering wheel. He was a man of action, always in control. He turned the red Ferrari around and headed back down the winding road toward the Grand Marina.

# CHAPTER 2

Sarina tensed in the seat next to Jason. Could he know? Why was he going back in the direction she was running from? Trying to hide the alarm in her voice, she asked, "Where are you taking me? Please, I want to go away from the marina."

"I am taking you someplace safe, where you won't have to worry about working. You'll have a warm place to stay until you can walk again. I have a house on the beach. You'll be safe there."

Sarina sat quietly as Jason drove down to the city, which had the same name as the island. The streets around the plaza were full of people all out having a good time. Along the coast road, with the smell of the fresh sea air and the wind blowing in her hair, Sarina tried to relax. He turned down a narrow road, the Ferrari taking up the entire width. The crunching of gravel was the only sound.

She hadn't seen a house for miles. Sarina wasn't worried about being alone with him. There was something about this man that made her feel safe.

Would she ever kiss another man without comparing

their kisses to this man's? His kiss left its mark on her lips… the feel of his mouth… the taste of his tongue. She would remember that kiss always.

He turned the car onto a dirt road, and she heard the surf. *How close to the water are we?*

He stopped his car in front of a magnificent home. Coach lights framed a large, sprawling three-story house with a manicured landscape and tall palm trees, the trunks lit by accent lighting. A fountain gurgled in the center of the stone walkway leading to double front doors. Lights were also on inside the villa. *This is a house? His definition of house is certainly different from mine.*

He came around and opened her door, then he took her hand to help her to stand. Her ankle throbbed, and her shoe felt tight on her injured foot. Sarina stood and winced, leaning against the car. He caught her, his muscular arm going around her waist. Jason steadied her as she balanced herself.

"Easy… let's see if you can stand on your own."

There was too much pain in her ankle. She tipped her head back and gazed up into his eyes.

"Allow me to carry you," he said as he lifted her up in his arms.

Sarina raised her arms around his powerful neck. She stopped herself from resting her head on his broad shoulder and caught the sigh that almost escaped her.

He carried her past the fountain and up the steps into the house. The entry foyer was massive, open to all three floors, with a round, stained-glass skylight in the ceiling. A large, round, marble-topped table stood in the center of the foyer, the only adornment a vase with an arrangement of fresh flowers, the fragrance of roses perfuming the air. Ornate gold-framed mirrors hung on the walls, and full-size Roman statues stood at the entry.

To the left, a staircase that she thought would be better suited to a palace led to the second floor. Past the stairs was the dining room, with its gleaming wood table and twenty-four high-back chairs. A crystal chandelier hung above the center of the table and on the walls, crystal sconces. Along one wall was a matching sideboard, and on the other side, double French doors led to a patio.

*This is a beach house? It's a mansion.* To the right of the entry, another set of French doors led from the living room to a separate patio. *Is that a grand piano in the living room?*

Sarina was uncomfortable as he carried her through the house and up the staircase. He walked down a vast hall, and at the end, the massive double doors were open. He stepped into the bedroom, and she saw a four-poster bed. Yards and yards of pale-blue netting hung from the posts, and a blue satin bedspread covered the mattress.

On one wall, a fireplace, the facade carved out of marble —she had never seen anything quite like it—the mantel was taller than her five feet three inches. The drapes on the windows were dusky blue, trimmed in gold. A burgundy watered-silk couch faced the fireplace framed by two wing chairs upholstered in blue velvet and trimmed with satin. The thick Persian rug in front of the fireplace had the colors of the drapes and was speckled with deep burgundy, cream, and gold. It was summer, and though they were at the water's edge, it was too warm for a fire.

Jason held Sarina around the waist and helped her walk to the massive bed. She sat near the footboard, with her hands folded in her lap. How would she ever get around? Maybe just a good night's sleep and rest were all she needed for her ankle to be better.

Her stomach rumbled. Her eyes widened, and she covered her mouth with the tips of her fingers.

Blue eyes, the color of the sky, looked at her in surprise. "When was the last time you ate?"

"I think yesterday on the plane," she mumbled.

"I'll be right back. I'm going to fill the tub."

He came back into the bedroom and walked over to her. "I'll make you something to eat. Do you think you can walk to the tub on your own?"

"Yes, I'm sure I can manage."

"Good. Now, go take a bath. Soak your foot." He was all business again. He seemed to be in his element when giving out commands.

"You're good at giving orders."

He offered a brilliant smile, showing even, white teeth, before he walked out of the bedroom, pulling the doors closed behind him.

Sarina wasn't sure if she could put any weight on her foot and walk. Right now, sitting on the bed, it didn't hurt. She moved her ankle, and pain shot up her leg. "Ouch. Will I be able to stand?"

She took off her canvas sandals. The wedge heel was too high for her to stand on. Once she took off her shoes, she could hobble into the bathing chamber. Stopping at the large arched entry, she gasped, "Oh my," glancing around the oval-shaped bathing suite.

The room was bigger than the entire apartment she shared with her widowed mother and sister Julia. One concave wall was floor-to-ceiling mirrors. A crystal chandelier with eight candelabras hung above the oval sunken tub, one that could comfortably accommodate a dozen people. She knew it would take quite a while for that monster to fill.

Sarina couldn't miss her disheveled appearance in the wall of mirrors, her face smudged with dirt. She had clipped her hair up, but now it was a wild mass of tangles and curls. Her blouse wasn't only ripped but covered in dirt. Her cream-colored slacks were torn at both knees and in no better condition.

The marble-and-glass shower had so many spray heads, she wasn't sure how to turn it on. Finally able to get the shower working, Sarina worked a thick lather into her hair, then she rinsed and washed her body. She wrapped herself in a thick bath towel, tucking the end between her breasts. *Bossy said to soak my foot, so I had better do that.*

Sitting at the edge of the sunken tub, Sarina was concerned that if she went into the tub with the pain in her ankle, she wouldn't be able to get out. The water felt good on the bruise, so she did soak it for a while. Then she went in search of something to wear. Not wanting to put on her dirty, ripped clothes again, they would have to be washed. She would also need a needle and thread so she could repair her blouse. The tears on the knees of her pants would have to stay.

She hesitated for a moment, then went into the wardrobe. There were only men's clothes. Her brows pulled together, and she gasped. *This is Jason's room!* She would have to make it clear that she wouldn't be sleeping with him. He may think differently by the way she had acted, practically gluing herself to him while he explored her mouth. Just thinking about that kiss made her warm all over. What was wrong with her?

What must he think of her and the way she kissed him back? Her nipples were getting hard now just thinking of his tongue in her mouth. When he crushed her to his hard, muscular chest, the juncture between her legs had pulsed.

She tried to clear her head of those thoughts and took one of the many shirts off a hanger and put it on, making sure to button it all the way down. She looked in the mirror and laughed at herself; the French cuffs went past her fingertips, so she rolled them up.

She hobbled back to the bedroom just as Jason knocked at the door and strode in. He carried a tray filled with all sorts of delicious-smelling food. He stopped to gaze at her.

~

HIDING the spark of desire in his eyes, he said, "I see you found something to wear. Tomorrow, I'll bring you some clothes that my sister keeps here." He put the tray on the coffee table by the burgundy watered-silk couch. She managed to walk over and sit. He lifted the crystal wine decanter and poured her a glass of red wine. Lifting the other glass, he poured one for himself as well.

He handed Sarina the plate with the omelet he'd made for her. On a separate platter, he'd put chunks of cheese, black and green olives, and crusty bread. Another plate held grapes, orange sections, and apple slices. He moved the plates closer to Sarina.

Jason sat in a wing chair opposite her, sipping his wine. *Does she know how beautiful she is?* Skin velvety smooth and like alabaster, no freckles. Deep-red hair drying into loose ringlets all around that angel's face. Her eyes framed in dark lashes took his breath away—emerald green. The same color as the emeralds his late mother loved to wear.

Sarina tugged the hem of his shirt down over her shapely legs. He knew she has some great curves. Petite and curvy, he had felt her more than ample breasts against his chest. He'd known the moment her nipples hardened, stabbing into his chest. Her well-toned, petite body was so different from his usual type. He wanted to feel her legs wrapped around him. She was nothing like the women he was used to. They were tall and thin, model thin.

He looked at her ankle and frowned. The delicate skin was purple and swollen. Bringing a footstool over from one of the wing chairs, he knelt to feel the ankle. He gently lifted her foot and propped it on the upholstered stool.

He gazed up into her green eyes. "I don't think it is broken, though it is quite swollen. You have to see a doctor."

"It's too late for a doctor. It must be after midnight—"

"Actually, it's two."

"Oh, later than I thought… In any case, I don't have money for a doctor visit."

He stood to his full six-foot-three height and frowned. "I said you need a doctor. I'm calling mine. He makes house calls. You can pay me back after you get that job at the palace." He reached into his tuxedo jacket pocket. Taking out his cell phone, he punched in a number. With the phone to his ear, he walked out of the room.

# CHAPTER 3

$\mathcal{S}$arina sat on the terrace looking out at the sparkling blue water of the Mediterranean and the white sandy beach below. The briny sea air soothed her. She wore one of Jason's shirts, her foot and ankle bandaged, an ice pack placed on the part most swollen. She reclined on a chaise lounge, sipping her morning coffee. On the low white-iron table by her side sat a sandy-colored china plate with a croissant and, next to that, a bowl of fruit.

*How on earth will I be able to work?* Luckily, the doctor Jason insisted come last night examined her ankle and told her it wasn't broken but badly sprained. She needed bed rest for at least a week. Impossible! Rest, ice, and elevation to help the swelling go down. *I don't have a week—I must get home.*

The doctor had left some pain pills. Sarina was always so reluctant to take pain meds. She hoped they wouldn't give her nightmares like the one other time she had to take pills for pain. She'd had terrible nightmares and talked in her sleep.

Her thoughts came back to her most pressing problem—

stranded in a foreign country with no money. You couldn't make this stuff up! *I'll have to tell Jason that I need to find a job.* She would need enough money for a one-way ticket back home. Without any savings to draw from, she had no other option than to find a job. Her widowed mother and younger sister relied on her income. Neither of them could wire her any money.

Now the salary she'd counted on to help at home would no longer materialize—since the companion position wasn't what she had expected. She shuddered, thinking back to the scene on the *Carmella* and the anger in Mrs. Williamson's eyes when she'd voiced her objections. *"You were aware of the position when we met. I know I made it abundantly clear to you... the type of escort I was hiring. Go below deck until I can sort this all out."* All she did was snap her fingers—

Jason cleared his throat. "You seem preoccupied."

She looked up, startled. He sat opposite her. Deep-blue eyes, the same blue as the sky on a cloudless day. She melted and averted her gaze. Tall, dark, and handsome, like a dream. Every woman's dream, or at least hers. His light-blue polo shirt stretched across a muscular chest, and two buttons were open, revealing his tanned neck, where a few dark hairs peeked out. The muscles in his arms made the palms of her hands itch with need, wanting to run them over him. She remembered the feel of those hard-as-steel muscles. His legs encased in faded jeans. Jason's hair was still damp from the shower he must have had before waking her. Sarina's mouth went dry. She swallowed and turned away. She would rather not get caught with a look of longing on her face.

He put his coffee cup and saucer back down on the table. "Today, you rest. The pain medication that the doctor prescribed for you is potent. You'll probably sleep most of the day." He came around to Sarina. "Let me help you get to the bed."

He scooped her up and carried her back into the bedroom, laid her on the cool sheets. He reached for the covers and brought them up so she could snuggle under the comforter.

"Sleep. I'll look in on you later. Then we'll put another ice pack on your ankle."

~

JASON WALKED FROM THE ROOM, gently closing the door behind him. *She's beautiful,* he thought, *with that angelic face. Petite isn't my usual type, but her curvy body is having an effect on me.* Jason couldn't forget the kiss they'd shared. It wasn't like him to be so caught up by a mere kiss. From the moment his hands touched her, his lips sliding over her sensuous ones, he couldn't stop thinking about her. The velvet softness of her tongue, timid at first—then she had become eager to play and have him explore her mouth. She'd fit herself fully against his chest, getting close… closer… She surrendered her mouth to his demands… He'd never felt that way before.

Jason mentally shook himself. His thoughts were concerning. *How can I be aroused so quickly by one kiss, aroused as never before—and with a single kiss? What has come over me?* Jason never reacted so quickly to a woman. He couldn't get enough. She felt good in his arms.

*Only sex that has always been my way and will always be. Lots of sex and lust, but never romance.* Jason shook his head as he walked into the adjoining bedroom. What was the reason for putting her in his bed?

Jason reached into his pocket, taking his phone out, and called his sister Catarina. They were close, and after their parents died, he'd raised her. Now, he called her so she wouldn't worry about him. He told her he wanted to stay at the beach house for a few days and didn't want to be disturbed.

"You deserve a break. I'll keep everything running smoothly. Love you, big brother." He knew Cat would understand. Ending the call, he walked out onto the terrace. Jason sat on the orange-and-white-striped cushion of the outdoor couch, stretching his arms across the back, crossing his leg and resting his ankle on his thigh. Gazing at the sea, he watched a sailboat in the distance. On the white sandy beach below, boulders were stacked, forming a border on one side of the house before jutting out into the sea.

He had worked hard to turn San Destino into the prosperous, thriving nation it was. That was how he'd become acquainted with Howard Williamson, the billionaire builder, years before.

Jason had interviewed Howard, explaining how he wanted to focus on tourism to transform San Destino. Jason's vision for the Grand Marina included adding more slips for larger yachts and building a new yacht club and adding ten more exclusive hotels that offered privacy and top-notch service to their wealthy guests. They built the hotels into the terraced landscape surrounding the marina.

Jason continued to develop San Destino's other resources, adding four more state-of-the-art hospitals to the island and two more airports. It made him a billionaire in his own right, and the people of San Destino had one of the best economies in the world, thanks to him.

His thoughts drifted back to the woman sleeping in his bed. He knew Sarina ran from Chad and Derrick. He knew the type of women they liked. Joanna Williamson certainly indulged them when it came to women, paid escorts of the highest quality. Doting Joanna handed Chad and Derek summer flings without any commitment.

The clothes he'd ordered for Sarina had arrived, and he

had the staff place them in the master bedroom dressing room. He knew from experience what women liked and what made them look good. He spared no expense with this one. She had the face of an angel and the body of a siren.

It was well into the afternoon when he went to check on Sarina. She looked lost on the enormous bed, curled up in a ball with the satin coverlet thrown to the side. One arm was tucked around the pillow, and her red hair flowed behind her. She still wore his shirt… He felt jealous of that piece of material, the way it caressed her skin, touched her breasts, curved around her buttocks. He wanted to run his hands on her ivory flesh and feel the satin texture. *Is the rest of her body as velvety smooth as her cheek is?* Looking at the bandaged ankle, he forced those thoughts out of his head.

He wanted her… He should have told her he'd had dinner on the *Carmella*. He remembered how she panicked when he drove in the marina's direction. Her fear was visible, though she tried to hide it from him. She'd sat rigidly on the seat next to him, then when he drove past the yacht, she'd turned and looked in the other direction. Her small hands had balled into fists before she opened them to lie on her knees. Her fear had concerned him, so he decided to keep the secret. Let her be the one to tell him when she was ready.

The sun had set when Jason knocked at the master bedroom door. He didn't wait for a response as he pushed the door open. He'd drawn the shades earlier when he'd brought her something to eat and put an ice pack on her ankle. Now, the room was in semi-darkness, and Sarina stirred in the bed. He walked in and adjusted the dimmer switch so that the lights gradually brightened.

～

Sarina pushed herself up on the bed, careful of her ankle, and adjusted her pillows. She finger-brushed her hair off her face. "Hi, what time is it?"

"It's early evening." Jason walked over to the bed and smiled at her. "How do you feel?"

"I'm a little groggy, but I do feel much better. Thank you."

"The pain medication can do that. How about a hot bath and then dinner? You must be hungry. I had some clothes sent here from town. They're in the dressing room. Let me show you."

He lifted her out of bed and carried her into the dressing room. One wall was now full of women's clothes. She saw a collection of clothes ranging from casual to formal. She guessed that they were his sisters. He set her down on a burgundy brocade fabric divan and brought over several gift boxes, handing the largest one to Sarina while he placed the other two on the marble-topped table next to her.

"What's this?" she said, unable to hide the amazement from her voice.

"I had some clothes sent over for you to wear. The sizes should be close enough."

Sarina opened the box on her lap, and between the folds of delicate, silver-toned tissue paper, the emerald-green silk fabric of a dress peeked through. She lifted the sleeveless boat-neck silk dress with trembling fingers. "Oh, this is beautiful." Then she opened the shoe box, and ran her finger along sexy gold flat sandals. The sides of the sandals were crystal, to look as if her foot rested on glass. She wasn't sure if she would be able to walk.

"I'll carry you for now."

Surprised that he must have guessed her thoughts, she looked up into his handsome face. She lifted the lid on the last box. A nude-colored, lacy bra, with matching thong panties, a garter belt, and silk stockings with a lace border rested on a bed of silver-toned tissue paper. Her face flamed when she saw the all-too-sexy lingerie. The sheer cup of the bra would only reach to the crests of her breasts. Delicate lace outlined the cup as well as the sides and the straps. A lace ruffle went entirely around the underside of the bra. The thong was sheer and would leave nothing to the imagination. Her cheeks were on fire, but she forced herself to face him with one eyebrow raised in question before she turned to him.

His smile dazzled her.

With a slight shrug of his shoulder, he said, "I thought you would like to wear something new rather than borrow my sister's lingerie."

"I appreciate that, but these are too fancy," *And flimsy.* She'd never worn a thong in her life!

"The clothes in this dressing room would have been good enough as long as your sister wouldn't mind."

He swept his arm out toward the garments. "These don't belong to my sister. They are yours."

Stunned silence filled the dressing room. Sarina couldn't utter a single word. She knew people didn't give you anything without wanting something in return. Hadn't she recently learned that lesson from Mrs. Williamson?

"I can't accept these. It's too much. I certainly cannot afford to pay you back." Her voice rose. "I told you I have to find a job. I need to purchase an airline ticket and go home."

"I haven't asked for money. Now have I?" His gaze held hers.

The meds were making her crazy. Wherever his blue-eyed gaze touched her, Sarina felt a stroke of fire on her skin. She averted her eyes, and in a softer voice, she said, "No, you have not."

He bent but didn't touch her. She lifted her gaze to his vibrant blue eyes.

"These are for you, no strings attached. Now, go take a bath and relax." He lifted her and carried her into the bathing chamber.

"I can't accept the clothes. I want to pay you for the items I must wear. I won't wear any if you don't let me pay you." Her voice was as firm as it could have been with him carrying her.

"I won't mind if you walk around naked." He teased her again. She looked up to see his brilliant smile and the crinkles around his blue eyes.

"Please, you have to understand—"

"Just accept these clothes, as I have said, no strings attached. Is that not the correct American expression?"

"Yes, that is. One day, I'll pay you back for the clothes that I must wear."

He smiled at her and continued into the bathing chamber.

This was crazy to be carried by him. Each time he came close, she just turned to jelly. Her brain couldn't form one clear thought. The feel of his powerful arms holding her and his scent—pure male swirled around her, making Sarina forget reason.

"Maybe you should have invested some money in a pair of crutches; you wouldn't have to carry me."

"Have I complained?" He turned on the shower. "Wear the dress to dinner," he said. Then on the way out of the bathing chamber, over his shoulder, he said, "I'll lay it on the bed."

She bathed, then wrapped herself in a large, fluffy towel and carefully made her way to the dressing room. The shower had cleared some of the groggy effects of the pain medication from her brain.

Jason had said that all the perfumes and makeup on the vanity were bought for her use. She marveled at the fact he had forgotten nothing. He knew women and how to please them; she was sure of that. He probably had to beat them off with a stick. Every single time he picked her up, she had to control herself and not pull his head down for a kiss.

That kiss… Her lids slipped down, almost closing over her eyes. She sighed at the memory of his kiss. The way it did crazy things to her. His height, his broad shoulders… his masculinity, that handsome face. She had to stop. Her nipples tightened, and heat spread between her legs, begging for him.

Sarina sat at the dressing table and wrapped the bandage around her foot and ankle. She wasn't one to wear much makeup, so she applied a small amount of mascara to her lashes. Sarina used a coral shade of lipstick, pinched her cheeks for some color, and was done. She pinned her hair up in a messy bun, then dabbed some perfume behind her ears.

She wasn't quite sure about the thong. Some of her friends wore them, and even her sister Julia owned several. Holding it up, she shrugged and slid it on. She put on the bra, looked at the silk stockings, and decided not to put those on over the bandage. The sandals were perfect; they were flat without a heel. She saw the label and the red sole and knew there was no way she could ever afford them. The dress bore another high-end designer label. What had she gotten herself into?

Sarina limped to the bedroom, where the silk dress laid across her bed.

Jason, in a navy-blue suit, accenting his tall muscular form, strode into the bedroom, startling her. She lost her balance. He was at her side in a second, his strong hands at her waist, steadying her. She tried to cover herself, one hand at the juncture of her legs and an arm across her breasts.

"No, Sarina, don't. You're exquisite."

Caught in the frilly lingerie, she felt her cheeks flame. He picked up the emerald-green silk dress and helped her into it. He gently turned her to zip up the dress.

"You are beautiful. Shall we go?"

"Yes, thank you."

He bent to pick her up, and she couldn't help saying, "You should have bought me crutches. I'm sure they would have saved your back."

He lifted her higher on his chest. "You're as light as a feather. Have no concern for my back."

She didn't have anything else to say as Jason carried her down the magnificent staircase and through the open French doors of the dining room to the patio. A table covered in rose-colored damask had been set with china and sterling-silver place settings. He sat her in an upholstered, high-back dining chair, then he poured her a glass of sparkling water.

"Water, because of the meds you're taking," he breathed in his sexy, deep voice.

SHE WAS able to look at him for the first time this evening without embarrassment. He was the most handsome man by far she had ever seen. It was difficult for her not to stare. Tall, yes, and those chiseled features of a Greek god, with eyes the color of a cloudless day, so vibrantly blue. Sometimes when he looked at her, they turned the deep blue of the ocean. His jet-black hair... he was magnificent, and his body... rock hard. The suit he wore, she was sure, had been custom made, fitting his broad shoulders and narrow waist. The fabric she couldn't even guess at.

He'd kept her glass filled with water and lemon slices while he drank wine. She didn't know what they ate. She was too busy looking at him, though she vaguely remembered salad, lobster, steak. Dessert was chocolate and yummy. After dinner, he carried her from the patio down the stone steps lined with potted plants and bougainvillea in shades ranging from the palest pink to a deep red.

He walked along the beach. They didn't talk. The moon was full, the sound of the surf against the shore like music. He turned his head and looked into her eyes. Her arms were around his strong neck as he pulled her closer. His sculpted lips found hers. Gentle and sweet at first, then more insistent as he ran his tongue along the seam of her lips. They opened for him. She wanted him to explore her mouth, run his tongue along her teeth and then slide in to stroke her tongue.

She was hesitant at first, but he knew how to fan the flames of her desire. The blaze grew and grew, and she turned in his arms, getting closer to him, touching her tongue to his.

Time stood still, as her breath mingled with Jason's. His powerful arms around her, his scent, cologne and virile man, she was swept away and could stay like this forever. Her abdomen clenched, and the place between her legs throbbed as sweet liquid fire spread. She melted in his arms. Her breasts swelled, and the nipples tightened.

Sarina had been kissed before, but never did she feel like this. Sarina surrendered herself to the blissful feelings he stirred in her. Heat swirled through her body and settled between her legs.

"Let's get you inside before you catch a chill."

Chill? She was on fire from just his kisses. He carried her into her bedroom and set her in one of the wing chairs, poured himself a brandy and her a non-alcoholic beverage. He ran his fingers through his thick, black hair.

Sarina had to ask, knowing it was a little too late, but she had to be sure. "Do you live here alone?"

"If this is your way of asking if I'm married?" He tilted his head and studied her before he lifted one broad shoulder in the slightest shrug. "The answer is no; I am certainly not married."

She stared into her glass, hoping he couldn't see the color rise into her cheeks. Maybe not married, but she was sure there were women in his life. She had to let him know that the most important thing for her right now was getting home. Tomorrow, she would ask him for help, be more insistent. For now, she just wanted to look at him.

"It's time for your pain medication." He handed her the pill and a glass of water.

She reached for the glass. "Thank you."

"Let me help you unzip that dress."

She turned her back to him. He unzipped the dress, then he brushed a kiss on the back of her neck, another kiss a little lower, and once more between her shoulder blades. Shivers ran up her spine.

"Good night," he whispered, with a slight kiss behind her earlobe. He walked from the room.

Sarina was sad and yet so happy that he left. She knew she had no willpower when he came near. She undressed and put on one of the nightgowns he had purchased for her. It was satin and lace. The bodice was sheer, in a light blue with spaghetti straps and one long slit on the right side. She climbed into the massive bed and fell into a deep sleep.

JASON STOOD in the bedroom next door. His jacket and tie were draped over a chair, his shoes and socks on the floor by the bed. Jason's shirt hung open to the waist, and he paced back and forth. He couldn't get the image of Sarina in those frilly scraps of lingerie out of his head. He'd seen other women in far less, and he had never reacted quite like this.

She was petite, yes, but perfection when he fitted her

against him. Her hourglass body, tiny waist, and hips flaring to shapely legs. Her breasts were large, but they fit into his hands so well. He needed to feel them without any covering, to run his hands and his tongue over those perfect orbs, kiss the tips, then suck the nipples into his mouth… and oh, so much more.

He pictured her wherever he looked, on the chair, on the bed. The reality of seeing her in his bed drove him crazy, and now… the image of her in those scraps of lace added to his lust. He couldn't carry her much longer without stripping her, throwing her on her back, and doing what he desired with her.

Jason wanted her naked under him, begging for him, only him. He would wipe away the memory of every other man she had ever been with. He wanted her for himself for as long as he desired. It took a will of iron not to go to her when he found her in that bra and thong sexier than naked skin. He helped her dress for his own peace of mind, so that he didn't carry her to the bed and bury himself in her. He imagined taking her on the beach, on the table at dinner, in the bath, in the shower, in her bedroom—his bedroom.

Why did he put her in his bed and not join her? He still didn't understand that. *Yes, you do.* Her ankle needed time to mend. Jason couldn't carry her any longer—tomorrow, he would have a pair of crutches delivered. He wasn't a man to just use women. He would be careful of her injury.

While at dinner on the *Carmella*, he learned that one of the paid companions Joanna hired for the summer couldn't be found. He was on his way home when he saw her stumble on the road. Jason swerved his car to keep from hitting her. He'd realized who she was and what she was. Chad and Derrick had almost found her when he decided to step in and protect her. Why hide her and not let them have her back? After all, they were paying for her services. Jason never used prostitutes and never paid for sex. He didn't enjoy one-nighters. He was selective in the women he took to his bed.

He had felt something primitive in giving her his protection. What was that all about? The fear he heard in her voice when they drove past the *Carmella*, he didn't like that. He wanted to protect her from men like Chad and Derrick, keep her safe always. A very unusual sensation for him. Never feeling so about a woman, he buried those thoughts even before they fully surfaced.

He poured himself another brandy. It was almost dawn, and still, he paced.

"No. No. Leave me alone. Jason, help me."

He ran from the room.

JASON RAN TO SARINA. She lay on the bed, thrashing and screaming. "Nooo, please no."

"Wake up, you're having a bad dream." He sat on the bed and dragged her to him, holding her, calming her. Soothing her with his deep voice, he said, "It's all right, I'm here. It was only a bad dream."

She calmed, then he said, "You were having a nightmare. Sarina, you're safe here with me, shh. I won't let anyone hurt you."

Sarina cried on Jason's chest. Her voice was muffled. "Oh, Jason, it was terrible."

"Shh, it's okay. I'm here with you."

Her body shuddered, and holding on to him, she sobbed, "He was on a horse," her voice snagged, "and he knocked you to the ground and, and stole me."

"Who did?"

"I don't remember. Please, just hold me, please."

Jason caressed her hair, the silky strands curled around

his long fingers. Sarina laid her head against his shoulder, and her open hand rested on his chest. He kissed the top of her head and felt the shudder that went through her body. His arms held her closer. Another shudder, and he heard the deep breaths she was taking as she calmed down.

He smoothed her hair and breathed in her scent, gardenia and a unique fragrance that was Sarina.

He pictured her naked. Images of her on his bed, with her red hair fanned out on the satin pillows. He rolled on top of that soft, lethal body, spreading her thighs, entering her. Those shapely legs wrapped around his waist.

He had to stop that!

# CHAPTER 4

*J*ason cleared his mind as his embrace gentled. His only thought was needing to soothe her. Sarina turned her face up to him, her emerald-green eyes full of unshed tears. Jason groaned and placed a light, comforting kiss on her soft lips. At the first touch of her sensual mouth… those full lips… his groin caught fire. He could not, would not, fight his desire for her. Jason's control evaporated in the heat of Sarina's lethal body.

He was a man used to taking what he wanted, and right now, he wanted Sarina. Jason tugged her onto his lap, dragging her knees apart so that she straddled him. He pulled her into him, and her breasts pressed into his chest, her excited nipples driving him on.

He opened her lips with his and began a tender exploration of her sweet mouth. Sarina sighed and relaxed in his arms.

Jason needed no more encouragement than the soft sound of her sigh. He had to taste and feel the satin texture of her neck. His lips skimmed along the slender, graceful column, drinking in her taste. Her scent intoxicated him. It didn't matter what she was or how she made her living.

His gaze roamed over her perfect breasts. The see-through lace covering the crests and her nipples pressed into the delicate fabric. He kissed the swell of bare skin above the bodice before he slid his mouth onto the lace-covered crest. He sucked her nipple through the fabric.

Her moan broke the silence as he slid the spaghetti strap off her shoulder, down her arms, baring her breasts. He dipped his tongue in the warm valley. He drew a bare nipple into his mouth and traced the bud with his tongue.

Sarina's fingers tangled in his hair, arching her body into him. He needed her naked to his touch. Jason coaxed the satin material past her waist. The gown slid down her body. His hands on the flare of her hips, fingers splayed he drew her closer, and her knees slid on either side of his hips, her heat against him. His cock grew.

Her mouth was so delicious as she fit herself on his lap, her fingers playing in the hair at his nape.

Naked breasts brushed against his chest. She whimpered.

Jason rolled over, moving her to the center of the bed, brushing the nightgown down the curve of her legs. Silently, it floated to the floor. He kneeled above her naked, more beautiful than he thought possible. Jason wasn't prepared for the rush of desire that shot through him. He wanted to take his time exploring her passionate body as he bent over her, forcing his control not to slip...

SARINA MELTED into his powerful embrace. Desire hot and wild zinged through her. She wanted to get closer to his mouth. She slid her hands into his open shirt over the tanned skin of his chest, into the smattering of black hair, feeling the muscles, like rocks sliding under his skin. She arched her body into him.

Jason groaned and flicked his tongue against the peak of her breast. Liquid heat settled between her legs. Another moan escaped her parted lips as fire scorched her stomach, her abdomen, her thighs wherever his hands stroked her.

His lips trailed kisses over her hip to her inner thigh.

Sarina burned. He blew on her sensitized skin, and shivers of bliss traveled up her spine.

He nudged her legs apart.

Sarina tensed, lifting her head off the pillow as she saw his jet-black hair at the juncture of her legs, his shoulders wedged between the thighs he'd so easily spread. She knew what he would do and groaned.

Jason rose up her body, kissing her belly to her breasts, reaching her mouth. His tongue sparred with hers as desire ignited once more. Her fingers slipped through his hair. She arched her body, rubbing her wet breasts against his chest. Her tongue slid over and around his.

His open palm brushed along her abdomen, sliding lower, lower. A burning need wet her as one long finger traced her seam. His blue-eyed gaze held her while he thrust his finger into her heated core.

A fevered moan escaped Sarina as his finger swirled deep between her legs. He took her mouth again, thrusting his tongue in. His finger in her core, his tongue in her mouth. She was wild with this new experience. Once more, Jason kissed his way down her body, stopping at her breasts, sucking first one nipple, then the other, while his finger slipped over and around her clit.

She couldn't think about what he was doing as his kisses slid further down her body. Once more, he spread her. Open to his mouth, she felt his lips intimately kissing her. His thumbs moved, spreading her open to his tongue. Her breath caught in her throat, and her thighs relaxed, allowing Jason the freedom to do what he wanted to her.

His tongue… "Ahh…" How he moved on her, sucking, licking, nipping.

She clutched at the sheets. "Ohhh, oh." Her abdomen curled, and her hips lifted to his glorious mouth.

His tongue pressed on her clit. Her hips lifted, and her hands moved into his thick, black hair. Her fingers grasped his head, loving what he did with his tongue. She was wild, having lost control. Mindlessly, she lifted her hips up to his mouth. He spread her, sending his tongue deeper. She clutched at his hair, holding him to her as she writhed against his mouth.

"Ahh," a deep moan escaped her, and without warning, waves and waves of incredible hot bliss pulsed through her core. Her head rolled on the pillow as ecstasy filled her.

"Jason, oh Jason," she screamed, "Jason, oh my God." Her eyes flew open, her body arched off the bed. He held her buttocks in his powerful hands and massaged her flesh as his marvelous tongue thrust into her core.

Her body writhed as heat radiated through her from her core up to her breasts, making her toes curl. His glorious tongue stayed where she needed it most, her buttocks still cradled in his powerful hands. Sarina experienced her first orgasm. No one had ever done that to her before.

She was glad it was him. She felt heavenly, too dazed to think. There was only Jason. Jason rained kisses over her belly, her breasts, licking her nipples. He kissed her neck, and tangling his fingers in her hair, he kissed her lips.

Jason moved from her, and Sarina felt lost, wanting to pull him back to her. She watched as he shed his clothes. He opened the bedside table drawer and grabbed a foil packet. He smiled down at her, and Sarina held her arms out to embrace him.

Jason kneeled over her. He took her hand and closed it over his erection. "See what you have done to me?"

Her eyes widened. He was huge. Steal encased in velvet.

Jason lay over her, nudging her knees apart. She reached up, needing his kisses, wanting to feel the incredible pleasure he'd given her again. Her eyes closed on a sigh. He entered her that first little bit. She couldn't believe how wonderful all of this was. He kissed her lips.

"Look at me," he murmured.

She opened her eyes.

He moved in a little more. "You… are… so tight."

Sarina gazed into his sky-blue eyes. She did what felt right, opening her legs wider.

Jason groaned, kissing her lips. Sarina wrapped her arms around his powerful neck. At the same time, he moved his hips and plunged into her, filling her.

The sudden pain surprising her, she cried out and pushed at his chest.

He froze above her.

"Sarina," he whispered. Raising himself up on his hands, he looked down at her. He felt the barrier break with the force of his entry and still couldn't believe what happened.

Her beautiful face grimaced in pain, as her eyes closed. He touched her cheek with gentle fingers and felt a tear. This couldn't be. Incredibly, she was a virgin! But she was a prostitute.

"*Cara mia*, shh, shh. I'm sorry, I didn't know. I promise it won't hurt anymore."

Sarina opened her eyes, and another tear slid down her cheek.

"Trust me to make it better," he whispered, keeping his lower body motionless while buried deep in her.

She sniffed. He kissed her brow. Kissing away the frown of pain, he tasted a salty tear. Jason kissed down the column of her beautiful neck, her sensitive collarbone, back up to her lips, slow kisses exploring her mouth. He smoothed the silky mass of red hair from her face, kissing her lips again, down to her breasts, licking the nipples, sucking one into his mouth.

Her hands moved from his chest to loop around his neck. Her fingers brushed his nape before they dug into his hair.

"Sarina, I promise, it will be better soon." He brushed a kiss on her parted lips. "I won't move until you say to. It'll be better, I promise."

Beads of sweat broke out on his forehead as he fought for control. He'd kissed her tears away.

Sarina gazed up, and Jason saw the flame of desire spark in the depths of her emerald gaze. "Jason, it's better now," she whispered.

He couldn't stop the smile that spread across his lips. Ever so slowly, he pulled out.

Sarina's brows came together, and her body followed him. He smiled and kissed the tip of her nose, then her lips, as he entered her again. She was so tight and hot; he wasn't sure if he could be gentle much longer. "*Cara mia*, tell me if I hurt you."

All he wanted to do was put her legs over his shoulders and bury himself as deeply as possible in her sweet body. He controlled his urge, fighting to get his passion in check, and moved slowly in and out, in and out.

Sarina was the one to change the pace, her movements increasing as her arms tightened around his neck. She rubbed her breasts on his chest, kissing his jaw. She lifted her leg to his hip. He held her other knee in the crook of his elbow, protecting her injured ankle. Jason pumped into her tight core.

Her eyes widened. "Oh Jason, so good," she panted.

He thrust faster and faster. She held onto his shoulders, her heel digging into his back.

"Yes," she moaned. "Oh yes, yes," she screamed as she met his thrusts.

He panted her name, his balls tightened, and he buried himself to the hilt in her hot, tight passage. Sarina shuddered, her pussy clenching him, and he erupted into her. No woman had ever felt so right. They were both breathing heavily, their bodies damp. He moved to her side, holding her in his arms. She rested her head on his shoulder, her red tresses wild. They fell asleep as the sun rose.

Jason woke up as Sarina moved in the circle of his arms. He tugged her closer, turning her so that he could kiss her lightly on the lips. He touched her breast, and the nipple tightened.

"Mmm, I thought it was a dream," she said.

The thrill of this virgin's response was a new emotion for him. Sex had become stagnant… almost stale. The women of his world were all the same. He'd lost the thrill and the anticipation a long time ago.

"Good morning, *cara mia.*" He nuzzled her neck.

"Good morning." The smile she gave him was brighter than the sun.

He had too many questions. He thought she was a prostitute and then to find a virgin in his bed? Time enough for answers later. Right now, he just needed to bury himself in her hot pussy.

Jason explored her mouth. He marveled at how quickly he was ready for her again. "Are you sore?"

She moved in his arms with complete abandon, holding nothing back. Sarina moaned. "No, not sore."

Jason rubbed the tuft of red hair and slipped his middle finger into her. "I can feel how ready you are." He reached for a condom.

Her eyes rounded as she watched him roll the latex on. He nudged her legs apart and smiled as he entered that oh-so-tight body of hers. "Tell me if I hurt you."

Her lids slid over her green eyes. "Mmm, you feel… wonderful." The corners of her lips rose into a smile.

She was hot and his. Jason did what he wanted to do the night before and lifted her legs over his shoulders, going as far into her tight core as he could. She was fire.

"Don't stop," she moaned.

He was buried to the hilt. Jason shifted his hips from side to side.

"Ahh, yes." She moved under him. Her head rolled on the pillow. "That feels

sooo… oh… oh."

"You're beautiful in your wild abandon, so tight and hot." He groaned. Her core clenched and unclenched around him, stroking his cock. It was almost more than he could stand. "Look at me, Sarina."

She opened her eyes as a deep moan escaped her, and he watched the emerald green in her gaze turn a deeper green as she climaxed. A flush spread to her swollen breasts. He licked the hard nipples, taking one into his mouth.

She moaned. Her knees slid from his shoulders to rest on the crease of his elbows. Jason continued his long, deep strokes, driving her on with his possession. He wanted more, pistoning into her. His deep thrusts filled her, stroking her g-spot.

She whimpered, "Jason, yes, yes." She climaxed once more.

He couldn't hold back any longer, exploding into her with his own powerful orgasm. They lay on the bed, breathing heavily, exhausted.

He dragged her to his side and kissed her damp brow, needing to hold her in his arms, something he never did.

When the sex was over, he was happy to get out of bed. He slept with his mistresses but none of the cuddling that he wanted with Sarina. *Because she was a virgin.* He pushed those thoughts out of his head.

Her red hair tangled around his hand and curled around her shoulders. Her eyes were closed, and a ghost of a smile touched her kiss-swollen lips.

"I'm going to take a quick shower and then get breakfast for us. You rest."

"Mmm, okay, but I'd like to soak in the tub."

He ran his knuckle along her flushed cheek. "I'll fill it for you." He rose from the bed and pulled the covers over her seductive body.

Jason went into the bathroom, turned on the tub for Sarina, and stepped into the shower. When he finished, he wrapped a towel around his lower body and walked over to the bed. Her eyes were closed, sooty black lashes laying on her cheeks. "Sarina."

Her eyes opened, and she looked confused, then gradually she smiled at him. "I must have dozed off."

"That's good. You need to rest. Can I see your ankle?" She nodded, and he moved the comforter, exposing her injured ankle. "You have a nice kaleidoscope of colors going on there. The swelling has definitely gone down." He touched the ankle with the tips of his fingers. "Is it painful?"

"No, it isn't."

He bent and kissed the bruise. "The tub is almost full. I turned on the jets so you can soak your ankle. Let me help you to the bathroom."

"Thank you. You've been so careful of my injury." Her cheeks reddened.

"When you're finished with your bath, we can have breakfast up here on the terrace." He lifted her and brought her into the bathroom.

"I'm going to get dressed and then get us some food."

"Lots of coffee for me," she said.

Jason nodded and gave her a gentle kiss before he left her to bathe.

Jason prepared breakfast and called the palace to have the beach house cleaned while he took Sarina out sailing. He wanted as much time as possible alone with Sarina before he sent her on her way. It amazed him to find her a virgin and such a passionate one. Sarina had no idea who he was, and that was precisely how he wanted to keep it until he bought her an airline ticket and sent her home.

The wild abandon she possessed was just the diversion he needed right now. Those other women he dated, including his most recent mistress, were all the same. The flame had gone out of his relationship before it had fully ignited. There was no longer any excitement. The women were in it for what they could get from him: clothing and jewelry. Some were obvious enough to admit they wanted marriage—never love.

He ran the fastest from them. Just last week, when he had told his latest mistress of only one month it was over, she seemed more interested in the velvet-and-satin-lined box containing a diamond and sapphire necklace, matching earrings, and bracelet. A fortune in gems. He had presented her with the deed to their Paris apartment as well.

The sex was just that, sex. No excitement, no passion, nothing like Sarina's hot abandon. He hadn't felt anything like what he and Sarina shared in a long time, maybe never. He was relieved to be rid of his mistress and free again. Now, he could explore Sarina's sensual body at his leisure. He wanted to keep his identity a secret from her for as long as possible.

Jason walked out onto the terrace where she sat. The morning light played in her luscious red locks. She wore a summer dress of pale yellow with an orange-and-red print splashed across it. The pattern brought out the fire in her hair and reminded him of the fire in her. Her emerald eyes sparkled, and her pink lips were fuller than usual. Kiss swollen from him. He liked that.

Sarina had wrapped the bandage on her ankle and wore sandals. She looked like an angel, a natural beauty. *Did she know how beautiful she is?* His groin heated. He wanted to take her right there in the chair where she sat. Clearing his thoughts, he placed the tray on the table and poured coffee into two cups. Then he served her part of the omelet he had made, along with some fresh strawberries.

SARINA REACHED FOR A BUTTERY CROISSANT. Picking off a flakey piece, she popped it into her mouth. "Yum." She chewed and then sipped her coffee. "I usually have yogurt and fruit in the morning. This croissant is a treat." *He's so handsome.*

Jason reclined on his chair, a slight breeze ruffling his hair. The memory of how he looked above her last night and this morning excited her.

He'd dressed for sailing. She could tell by the white shorts and a navy-blue pullover shirt that molded to his muscular frame, with the collar open. His broad shoulders... *Does he have my nail marks on his back?* His narrow waist... The shorts were pulled tight across his muscular thighs. He wore rubber-soled deck shoes.

Jason placed his cup on the table. "Sarina, will you tell me what you were doing when I found you?"

Her head snapped up, and she gazed into his blue eyes. *Oh dear, I can't lie to him, but what would he think if he knew? So foolish of me to believe I could make that much money for doing nothing.* "You mean when you almost ran me over."

He lifted an eyebrow. "You know I didn't do any such thing."

Sarina smiled and lowered her gaze, then she placed her cup on the table next to his. She took a deep breath and slowly let it out, then she folded her hands in her lap. She leaned back against the cushions. "I'll need to start at the beginning. You see… I'm a kindergarten teacher from a small town in Connecticut. I live with my mother and younger sister Julia. My mother became disabled shortly after my father died. Between her hospital bills and… the funeral bills for my father, it… took all his life insurance and what little savings my parents had. Mom had to sell our family home, and with the economy being as it is, we moved into a two-bedroom apartment."

Sarina grinned. "Your bathroom is bigger than our entire apartment. My sister has a small part-time job and will graduate from college next year. I was planning ahead. Medical school is expensive. Student loans have become difficult to get… and financial aid." She shrugged a shoulder. "Well, I guess we aren't poor enough. I'm paying off my college loans. The small salary I make from teaching, along with my mother's monthly disability check, isn't enough to support the three of us."

Sarina shifted uncomfortably in her seat. "Last summer, I worked as a camp counselor, and this summer, I planned on accepting a teaching position in Alaska… but… then…" She sighed. "I read an ad on the internet. It said, 'Cruise the Mediterranean, live aboard a private yacht, as a companion. All expenses paid. Enjoy exciting destinations. Call for details.' I called… It sounded too good to be true. More than four times the money I make in a year at my job—for just two months of the summer—it was incredible. Airfare to and from…" Her voice drifted for a moment.

Jason leaned forward. "Go on."

"I met Mrs. Williamson at her home in Greenwich, Connecticut, for an interview." Sarina shook her head. "She seemed so nice and down to earth. I knew of the family and their social status. So, when she offered me the position, I accepted. I didn't know or suspect anything out of the ordinary, only a companion for her… I had no clue."

Jason nodded.

"When school ended, my airline ticket was delivered. I said goodbye to my mom and sister and boarded the plane."

Sarina looked at Jason and shrugged again, still not believing what happened next. "The little money I had on me is gone, along with my luggage and purse."

She took a breath. "I can't afford the airfare. I found myself stranded in a foreign country. I managed to sneak off the *Carmella*—that's the name of their yacht—and walked. You know the rest. I had to get away from them, find a job, and buy a ticket home. I was hiding when you found me." She sighed.

Jason leaned toward her. His spicy scent drifted on the slight ocean breeze. He touched her cheek with gentle fingers, and his thumb brushed her lower lip. "You're safe here with me. Don't think of anything but resting your ankle today. The yacht is probably gone by now."

Sarina pressed her cheek into the warm palm of his comforting hand. "Yes, you're right."

"You need to let the meds do their job. I do believe that some fresh air would be good for you. Have you ever been sailing?"

"No, never. I live near the coast back home, but no."

"After breakfast, we can take the sailboat out."

Sarina changed into a red bikini and wrapped a matching

sarong around her waist. She slipped into a pair of sandals and tied her hair into a ponytail. Jason took the sailboat out some distance from the shore. "There's a secluded cove up ahead. We can drop anchor there."

Sarina held a small picnic basket and blanket in her arms while he carried her to the white, sandy beach. He helped her stand near a palm tree while he laid out a blue-and-white gingham tablecloth and placed the wicker picnic basket on top.

Jason stepped out of his shorts. The thrill of seeing him clad in bathing trunks and top overwhelmed Sarina, along with his narrow waist, his powerful thighs, and his long, muscular legs. He lifted his shirt up over his head. A well-defined, tanned abdomen came into view. Her mouth went dry as she looked at his muscular chest, not hairy, but oh so perfect, his abs… Now, she knew what it meant when some of her girlfriends talked about their boyfriends having a six-pack. His was almost more with a narrow line of black hair running down the center, disappearing into his trunks.

Sarina remembered how his hair teased her breasts, and her nipples tightened. She averted her gaze. *All I can think about is his lovemaking and how I want him again.*

JASON STOOD. "Let's go in the water," he said without turning to see if she followed. Jason dove into the cool, refreshing Mediterranean. He had to control himself. *Am I a schoolboy? I can't get enough of her lethal body.*

He swam a short distance and came back quickly, knowing that she couldn't swim. She could hardly walk. He wanted to stay in the shallow water for her.

Sarina limped up to him. Jason pulled her into his arms,

shook his head, sending droplets of water spraying her. She laughed, and he bent down to kiss her lips.

He pressed his erection into her belly. She glanced up at him with rounded eyes.

"Are you surprised?"

They were waist deep in the water. Jason bent to take her mouth with his as their kisses grew more insistent. Jason slid his tongue across hers, and his hands moved to her buttocks, lifting her to his erection. Her shapely legs wrapped around his waist, and her arms went around his neck, her fingers running through his hair, caressed his nape.

*Hot, passionate virgin.* He slid his hand between them into the band of her red bikini bottom, over the tight curls. He slid one finger into her core and used his thumb to rub over her clit. She grew slippery at his touch, ready for him. He slid his finger in and out, going deeper, keeping his thumb on her clit. Sarina wrapped her legs tighter around his waist, moaning into his mouth. He curled his finger on her sensitive g-spot, needing to give her the most pleasure.

His mind chanted, *Slow down, slow down.* He couldn't take his own advice. She climaxed there in the water, wrapped around him. He watched her in the sunlight, feeling her climax and hearing her cry out her pleasure. Her head was thrown back, her neck exposed to his lips. Her complete abandon was glorious. Jason held her limp body against him.

She sighed and kissed his neck. "I feel greedy."

"There's no greed in this. Later in the boat…" he said and kissed her temple. He carried her back to the blanket. Sarina reclined on her side, propping her head up on her hand.

Jason lifted the lid on the wicker picnic basket, handing Sarina a china plate and a linen napkin. She sat up and draped the napkin across her lap. "We have several varieties of cheese and crusty bread, an olive salad, marinated peppers, and grape tomatoes." Taking two crystal wine glasses from the basket, he said, "I brought sparkling water for you. Nothing stronger with the pain medication you're taking."

Sarina nibbled on a piece of cheese and sipped her water. Then she fed him some olives. He took her hand and brought it to his lips as he licked her fingers of the juice. For dessert, they had fresh, plump purple figs.

"Do you live on San Destino year-round?"

"Yes, this is my home."

"Your accent, although slight... but—nonetheless—is not American or British."

"The official language of San Destino isn't English. I studied abroad and in the United States."

"You mean like boarding school?"

He didn't want to talk about this. "Did you always want to be a teacher?"

She laughed. "I'm sorry if I asked too many questions. And yes, I've always wanted to teach."

He caught her lips in a soft kiss. She lay in the cradle of his arms, and they spent the afternoon on the beach, lying on the gingham cloth under a blue sky.

"How does your ankle feel?"

She wiggled her toes and moved her ankle. "Much better."

Sarina lifted her hand and ran her fingers through his hair. "You know your eyes make the sky look pale."

He smiled at her, tucking a strand of her flaming-red hair behind her ear. The only sound was the water lapping at the shore and the sailboat gently rising and falling on the waves. Far off in the distance, Jason watched as two motorboats crisscrossed on the open ocean.

He held her in his arms, and she rested her head on his lap. Sarina fell asleep under the shade of the palm trees. *When was the last time I did anything like this? A picnic on the beach— Never. Hold a woman in my arms to comfort her? Never.*

Jason enjoyed this time with Sarina. She had no idea who he was, and that served his purpose. He was so used to people that only wanted from him. Oh, he would tell her sooner than later, but he didn't want to see her change when she found out. He wanted to protect her and keep her safe until it was time for her to go home and he back to the demands of his life. She was an innocent.

He could be away for a month, but not much more than that. Though August was Europe's vacation time, on his calendar was the marriage of his cousin Crown Prince Carlos. He had this part of June and all of July before the wedding. He decided in his autocratic way that he would keep Sarina and then, at the end of July, send her home. They would stay at the beach house, and he could go to his office periodically and take care of matters that needed his attention. His sister and her husband could handle all the other duties for a month.

SARINA COULDN'T BELIEVE how easily she fell into his bed. He was magnificent. She had no restraint when it came to his lovemaking. She wished she weren't such a pushover for his... virile body and his all-consuming, erotic lovemaking.

He was very autocratic, giving orders and in complete charge of every situation. He expected instant obedience when he spoke. Was he the CEO of a corporation? Her principal at the elementary school she taught at was the same way. Sarina wanted to know what his profession was. She knew he would help her go home.

Her thoughts tumbled one over the other. How could she again ask him for help? He bought her all those clothes. She would only wear a few so that he could return the rest and get his money back. She would pay for what she wore. He didn't offer to pay for an airline ticket, but he said he would help her. Now that the prospect of the summer job turned into a disaster, she needed to get home. Today she could put more weight on her injury when she tried to walk. She could wait until her ankle was fully healed.

Days went by, and the time needed for her ankle to mend was almost at an end. Jason was very loving. He made love to Sarina each night and during the day. He had all the latest films. Sometimes, they would watch a movie lying in bed or other times in his home theater. He made popcorn, and they would share the warm buttery kernels from the same cup.

He taught her to play chess. She mastered the game quickly and beat him several times.

She told him about her family and her life back home, how much she loved teaching and how proud she was that her sister Julia wanted to become a doctor. She would do anything to help her dream come true. She'd mentioned hot wings and beer.

He'd laughed. "I thought you were a pizza girl."

"I like sausage pizza."

They swam in the pool, Jason telling her it was better than the ocean—he didn't want her to hurt her ankle again. He felt it wasn't strong enough, and she agreed that she needed more rest.

Her ankle was completely healed now, and Sarina approached the subject of returning home. She had to get back to her mother and sister. First, she needed to earn money for the airfare and pay him back for the clothes he gave her. She wouldn't accept charity from him.

They were going out to a restaurant at the Grand Marina. Sarina wore her favorite dress, the green silk. She sat at the vanity in the dressing room, putting the finishing touches on her makeup.

Jason walked in holding a large, rectangular velvet box. "I

have something I hope you'll wear tonight." He lifted the lid on the box.

"Oh my, Jason, they're beautiful." She couldn't help running her finger along the earrings. A pear-shaped emerald hung from a huge round diamond. On the matching pendant, from a diamond twice the size of the earrings, hung a pear-shaped emerald on a white gold, diamond-encrusted thick chain. He placed the box on the vanity and removed the necklace. Sarina hesitated.

"Come, let me see this on you." She turned in her seat, and the cold metal touched her neck. She lifted her hand to hold the diamond and emerald pendant in place while Jason latched the chain to the back of her neck.

"So, what is it exactly that you do?"

He brushed kisses along her neck and shoulder. "You mean besides this?"

She looked into the mirror.

He held her gaze. "You're on your own with the earrings."

She was happy to wear the extravagant jewels for him. Once the earrings were on, she stood, picked up her wrap, and they left the house. They drove down to the restaurant in Jason's red Ferrari.

"You said that you went to Yale for graduate school. Where did you get your undergraduate degree from?"

"In England. I don't want to talk about that. One day soon, I'll tell you who I am and what I am." He shifted gears, slowing the Ferrari as it approached a sharp curve.

*That sounds ominous. Who I am and what I am.* "I believe you when you said you're not married or committed to anyone. I'm not happy that you won't tell me more, but I can wait." *Deep down, I do trust him. His gentleness and his caring can't be a lie.*

Jason parked the car and came around to open her door. When they entered the restaurant, the maître d' bowed low, but before he could address Jason, Jason greeted him as an old friend. The maître d' walked them through the restaurant. All heads turned to look at him.

He held out the chair for her to sit, and Sarina whispered, "So, it isn't only women who stop and stare."

"Don't you know it's your beauty that causes heads to turn?"

She ignored his comment as she looked around the restaurant. They were seated upstairs in an open-air room with arched, glassless windows along one side, overlooking the marina. The tables were situated in such a way that each party was given complete privacy. Candlelit sconces on the walls illuminated the room. Jason ordered for them without looking at the menu. She could drink now, so he ordered champagne.

# CHAPTER 5

On the drive back to the beach house, Sarina was mellow and completely relaxed. Jason came around and opened her door. He held her hand as she got out of the car. Their fingers intertwined, and they strolled into the foyer. It astounded her that he called this mansion a beach house. She couldn't believe it. They went up to the bedroom that she now shared openly with him. He led her out to the adjoining terrace and brushed a soft kiss on her lips.

Sarina raised a hand to his chest, the silk of his shirt smooth against her palm. She stopped him. "I realize you're a wealthy businessman. I believe you when you say you aren't married or attached in any way. Won't you tell me who you are?"

"I will soon. Right now, I just want you. Let us not spoil the mood with talk." He moved her hand from his chest to the back of his neck. "Much better," he said as he bent to her, taking her lower lip into his mouth, running his tongue along her teeth.

Sarina opened her lips to his kisses. She rose on her toes to fit better into his lean, hard body, holding him to her as he explored her mouth. She did prefer this to talking. The pulsing between her legs confirmed that. His tongue swirled around hers, twining and sparring, retreating. She followed, and he sucked on her tongue. His hands skimmed up her back, the only sound the slide of the zipper separating the silk fabric down her back, slipping her arms out of the dress. Her nipples tightened.

Jason's hands trailed fire over her skin as the dress fell to the floor to pool around her feet. His big, powerful hands slid to her buttocks, massaging her flesh, first one cheek, then the other. Heat coiled through her, the throb of need beginning deep in her core.

"You are beautiful." He'd pulled her into his erection, his lips hovering over hers as he took her mouth. He unhooked her bra and licked her collarbone across the top of her breasts.

She slid the straps of her bra down her arms, needing his mouth on her breasts. He circled one of her pointed nipples with the tip of his tongue, then sucked it into his mouth.

Her knees buckled, and Jason's embrace tightened while he treated the other breast to the same torturous, scalding heat. She held back a moan. He lowered himself to his knees, continuing his downward tribute on her heated skin. He swirled his tongue in her navel, his powerful hands on her hips as he thoroughly explored… lower… lower.

She gasped, moving her hands on his shoulders, digging her fingers into the fabric of his suit. Jason slid the scrap of lace thong to one side and kissed her. His searing, teasing tongue sunk into her, kissing her where she needed to feel him the most. She could barely stand it.

Sarina was wild with the pleasure he always brought her. Pleasure that until recently she didn't know existed. His tongue drove her on, and she reached behind her back to the silk bow that laid above the crease of her buttocks and untied her thong. Jason slid the fabric off her, leaving the garter and silk stockings on. He slid his hands up the back of her legs over the stockings to the naked flesh, stopping only when he reached her buttocks. He nudged her forward, moving his tongue into her heat, finding her essence. *Oh, I love what he's doing to me. His tongue is magic.*

He fanned the flames of her desire, licking and sucking her in all the right places. She was mindless, writhing, on his mouth as his tongue thrust into her.

As the first ripple of excitement rushed through her core, she whimpered. Frantic in her need, she cupped his head, and her fingers dug into his thick, black hair, holding him to her. Wild and insistent, Sarina was carried away by the waves of her climax. Jason stayed with her, prolonging the pleasure. In a euphoric daze of incredible bliss, her eyes closed on a sigh, she whispered his name.

Jason stood, lifting her into his muscular arms. He cradled her to his chest and carried her into his bedroom.

She lay naked in his arms, her head resting on his shoulder, as he carried her to the bed. *I crave what he does to me. He makes me want him without thought of anything else. I've never done anything like this, and now I feel that I can't live without him.*

Jason yanked his tie off and shed his clothes. Gloriously naked, his arousal jutting out at her, he came to the bed.

"You have too many clothes on," he said.

She helped remove her garter, sliding her silk stockings down her legs. He slipped her shoes off, and each thudded on the floor.

He reached for a condom, and her core pulsed, ready for him again. He was naked and handsome, his jaw set as he crawled over her. Sarina lifted her arms, her hands on his biceps. She lifted her head, and his lips found hers as his knee nudged her legs apart.

"I can't wait another second to be in your tight heat." Inch by magnificent inch, he pressed into her. She was slick, so wet for him. He stretched her, filling her with his huge male erection. Sarina looped her arms around his neck, tugging him to her.

"Jason. Oh, Jason. Yes. Yes. More, please."

He lifted his torso, locking his elbows as his deep thrusts filled her with rapture. She lifted her hips to meet his downward thrusts. Her legs wrapped around his waist. She held him to her as his deep thrusts filled her.

She arched her back, and Jason took a nipple into his mouth, sucking hard. Her panting ended in a scream as she pulsed around his hard-as-steel erection, feeling her climax rip through her.

"You're mine," he bit out, climaxing with her.

In the morning when Sarina awoke, Jason was gone from the bed. She showered and dressed. Vaguely, she remembered his words. She was in a fog of bliss when he'd said she was his. The words didn't upset her or frighten her. He'd held her to him, kissing her temple, her brow, then he tucked her head under his chin, and she fell asleep in his arms.

Now that she could walk again, she explored the house. She thought Jason had done all the cooking for them, though it looked as if someone came in to clean and keep the pantry well stocked.

*Maybe I can do the cleaning to earn money for my airfare. I'll have to talk to him about that.* Jason had convinced her to wait until her ankle was fully healed. He had said that sitting on an airplane for ten or eleven hours would only cause her discomfort, so she had agreed. Life and responsibility didn't stop; nothing had changed. She would have to get home and find another summer job.

Julia had taken a second job in a dermatologist's office for the summer. Evenings and weekends, she worked at the local mall to make extra money. She hoped her mother and sister were doing well. They would be worried if they knew what had happened to her. Cell phones were a luxury in the Moore household. They each had one, but certainly no international calling or texting. She hadn't even bothered to bring her little flip phone with her.

Sarina walked out the back door of the kitchen in search of Jason. His car wasn't where he had left it last night. She went to the garage. No car there. Where could he have gone? She went back into the living room. There were no personal photos anywhere in the home, though beautiful oil paintings hung on the walls throughout.

She heard a car. Only Jason ever drove on the narrow gravel road that led to this secluded mansion. Jason was back. She was sitting on the sofa in the living room when he walked in, handing her an arrangement of the most fragrant gardenias as he sat next to her.

"Oh, they're so beautiful. Thank you… How did you know I love gardenias?" She buried her nose into the bouquet. "Mmm."

"I saw you stop to smell the ones in the garden." He smiled and rubbed the lobe of her ear between his thumb and finger. "Your ankle looks better. I thought we would take a ride along the coast road. There's an out-of-the-way restaurant that makes the best local fare on the entire island."

Sarina bit the corner of her lower lip. She had to broach the subject now before she lost her nerve. "Jason, can we please… I need to talk to you." She took a deep breath and sat up straighter. "I'll work to earn the money for a ticket home… Will you help me? My mother can't wire me money or buy my ticket. I managed to keep my passport. It's upstairs in the vanity drawer."

His arm went around her shoulder. "I'll take care of you, you know that. At the end of the summer, you can go home.

You would be gone all summer. Stay with me until then." He shifted on the sofa, taking her hands in his. "Let us explore these newfound feelings we have. We both need to do that. I'll take care of you just as I have been. No worries about money. I've provided for you and will continue to do so."

She stiffened, the misery of a minute ago gone, replaced by anger as she looked at him. "What do you want me to be? Your mistress?" She stood and stamped her foot, then she turned to face him. "Just because I let you make love to me, you feel that you have the right to keep me here? Prevent me from going home? I want to go home. Loan me the money for a ticket or help me find a job. I have responsibilities I cannot turn my back on. I won't stay here against my will."

In his smooth, silky voice, he said, "Am I keeping you against your will? We both know that isn't true. Stay with me a little longer. We have so much more—"

*"You're mine."* His words niggled the fringes of her mind. He said it so calmly, as if it were his right to dictate to her. Sarina looked into his vibrant blue eyes. "I have to get home. You know how important it is to me."

"Let's talk about it over dinner." His voice sounded like a caress. "Get ready." The tender tone hid the command it was as he continued, "We'll have a nice dinner and enjoy each other's company."

Sarina knew it was just sex for him. What did she expect, the way she practically threw herself at him? She had no sexual restraint when it came to Jason. He knew why she had come to San Destino. Did she think he'd fallen madly in love with her, just because she was so in love with him? *Love? Why did I think that? Of course he doesn't love me. I trust him not to hurt me. But love...* She had to get away from him and go home. Each day she stayed made it more difficult to end it.

He would leave her, anyway. She knew he didn't love her. Despite the ping pong her mind played, she knew beyond reason that she did love him. She had from the beginning. With just one look from those blue eyes, all her determination vanished. She had to get home and try to salvage part of the summer.

SARINA MADE up her mind to take matters into her own hands. The first chance she had, she would sneak away and go to one of those jewelry stores she'd seen the other night when they had dinner at the Grand Marina. She would sell the emerald and diamond jewelry he'd given her to wear. Then she'd go home and send him the money a little at a time until she paid him back for the clothes she did wear as well as the jewelry. All she knew was that she was getting deeper into debt each day, monetarily and emotionally. She couldn't let her heart dictate any longer. She would have to walk to the Grand Marina. Would she have enough time to sell the jewelry and then get to the airport?

For now, Sarina decided she would enjoy Jason's lovemaking. The memories would have to last her a lifetime. Deep down in her soul, she knew there would never be another man for her. Europe did crazy things to her, like walking off the *Carmella* without a dime and only the clothes she wore and now thinking of selling his jewelry so she could run away from him.

They drove to another secluded restaurant, high up in the hills of San Destino. The parking lot was almost empty except for his car and two others. He opened her door, taking her elbow, leading her into the restaurant. The host sat them at a corner table away from the other two couples.

She'd pinned her hair on top of her head in a messy bun. Her teal-colored bandage dress molded to her curves like a second skin. She wore the pear-shaped emerald earrings on her ears, and around her neck, the round diamond with the attached pear-shaped emerald hung on a white-gold chain. The jewel nestled between her breasts.

Jason wore a charcoal-gray suit with a crisp white silk shirt. The tie around his neck was the same color as his eyes. "Eat," he said. "Have I told you how beautiful you look?" He leaned in and whispered, "You make me want to lay you on the table and dine on you."

She blushed. It had become easier for her to understand his love talk or, as he called it, sex talk.

She lowered her fork, unable to swallow past the knot in her throat. Leaving him wasn't an easy decision. She'd made up her mind, but she felt vulnerable and confused. He'd left her no choice.

Sarina couldn't stop thinking about him. His lovemaking was a brand on her body as well as her heart, something she couldn't easily turn away from.

"You know I have to get home. It would be easier for me to go now since my ankle is fully healed."

He reached across the table to hold her fingers. "Before you go, let's spend some time exploring the island. This is your first trip out of your country, so let me show you around."

*He is so smooth.* "I wish you would tell me about your life here… and your work."

He shrugged his shoulders and smiled at her. "What is there to tell? Not very much. I would rather talk about you."

"I've told you everything."

She felt strange on the drive back along the winding road that led down to the beach house. She had to try one more time to have him see the urgency in her situation.

He was so carefree. That was the difference between the two of them. He gave her expensive jewelry and expensive clothes! Sarina's thoughts spun around and around, torn between her responsibilities at home and the freedom to be as carefree as Jason.

He kept something from her. She was positive about that, but at the same time, she was so confused by all that had happened. There was more that she didn't understand. What was the dark secret?

She knew what she had to do—run away from him and get home. He left her no choice.

# CHAPTER 6

*J*ason had dressed impeccably, as always, in a gray silk suit. The crisp white shirt brought out his suntanned skin. The tie around his neck—gray with thin, navy stripes and thicker sky-blue stripes—brought out the color of his eyes. At his wrists, white-gold cufflinks glinted in the sunlight that streamed through the window as he brought the china cup to his sculpted lips.

"Good morning, beautiful. An unavoidable matter arose, and I'll be out most of the day… possibly into the evening."

"So, you do work," she said, pulling the silk dressing gown tighter around her waist. "You just don't want to tell me what it is you do."

He smiled at that and said, "Tonight, I'll tell you, but for now, I must go. You can have a nice, quiet day. We'll go to dinner when I return." He kissed her cheek.

Sarina knew she couldn't waste any more time. When would another opportunity such as this arise? She raced up the grand staircase to the bedroom and into the dressing room. She found her old clothes, the ones she wore when she left the *Carmella* among the new clothes he'd given her. They were dry cleaned and the rip on her blouse mended. She dressed, thinking there would be plenty of time to walk into town and sell the jewelry. Sarina grabbed her passport out of the vanity drawer, and with a determination she didn't think she possessed, she dashed out of the breathtaking beach house and Jason's life.

The early morning breeze blew through her hair, turning it copper as she walked toward the town. The sea sparkled like winking diamonds against the strip of white sand, colorful blankets and umbrellas dotting the beach. Some people lazed in the sun, while others frolicked in the water. What little she saw of San Destino was beautiful. She turned down a narrow, cobblestone street toward the marina. It was full of people milling about, going in and out of the boutiques, some carrying bags with designer names on them, others eating a gelato or having an espresso.

Sarina stopped at the very first jewelry store she came to and was buzzed in. "*Salve*," said the man behind the counter.

"Hello, do you speak English?" Sarina asked.

"Si. Yes, but of course I do. How may I help you?"

The jeweler's eyes widened when she placed the earrings and pendant on the glass-topped counter. He seemed happy to give her what she thought was a fair price. The money was more than enough for the airfare home.

"Would you mind calling a taxi for me?"

"Yes, right away. Where shall I say you wish to go?" the man asked.

"To the airport."

SARINA SAT in the airport terminal. Surprisingly, the flight home would board in forty-five minutes. Those minutes were the longest she ever had to endure. As she tried to relax in the metal bank of seats at her gate, Sarina's thoughts raced.

She hadn't left Jason a note. What would she say? *I'll never forget you*—just thinking about those words almost stopped her from her plans. It was bad enough how sad and uneasy she felt when she sold the precious stones. She knew they had to be more valuable than what she'd asked the jeweler for. Sarina already felt all kinds of rotten leaving him, but he left her no choice. She had to get home.

Sarina was proud of herself, amazed at how it all went so smoothly, although she hated leaving Jason without even a goodbye… She knew she would never forget him, but how could Jason believe she would willingly stay without any independence of her own? Her wishes had to mean something to him.

Twenty minutes.

She thought of her family, her mother, her younger sister Julia. They didn't live frivolously and weren't extravagant. Just the basics. No luxuries, a roof over their heads, food, and clothing. Her car was almost as old as she was. How would she help her sister pay for medical school? Sarina had her own student loans to pay, but helping Julia become a doctor was something she had to do.

Her mother had warned her that the summer job sounded too good to be true. Her mother's words echoed in her head: "Why would anyone pay so much money for a companion? Look into this in a little more detail, honey. You've always been too trusting of people." Well, she made a mess of things now, her life included.

Fifteen minutes.

In the beginning, she depended on Jason because of her ankle, but now, he had to realize she couldn't just stay because he wanted her to. Who did he think he was, anyway? He was so autocratic; it made her wonder, was he always used to getting his way? She wished that things could have ended differently with him sweeping her off her feet, professing his undying love. She rolled her eyes at her thoughts.

The circumstances that brought them together were almost unbelievable. He wasn't the type of person she'd have ever met in her small world.

Sarina glanced at the large, round clock on the wall above the airline clerk's counter. Any minute, they would begin boarding. She watched as five men in police uniforms approached the desk.

Panic struck her, and she sat there holding her breath. *Oh, just calm down. It could be for any reason. Jason wouldn't even be home yet, and you left no note. He would just think you went for a walk. This isn't about you.*

The clerk pointed in Sarina's direction. *Oh dear!* Sarina's heart beat a little faster. The officer who seemed in charge stood directly in front of her. The other four split up, two to the right and two to the left of her. *Where do they think I'm going?*

The officer directly in front of her spoke. "Are you Sarina Moore?"

"Yes, I am, sir."

"May I see your passport, Madame?"

She reached into her pocket, removed the passport, and held it out to him.

He opened it, looked at her photo, and said, "Miss Moore, please come with me."

"Can I ask the reason?" Her voice was surprisingly steady.

"You are under arrest." His was calm, almost matter of fact.

"What is the charge?" Her voice wasn't as calm as she would have liked.

"The charge, Madame, is a theft of emerald earrings and an emerald pendant."

She knew that. The part that completely staggered her was when he said, "These are part of the Crown Jewels. You'll be taken to the palace where His Majesty King Filippo will formally charge you."

Crown Jewels? The king? She was in more trouble than she thought possible. Her legs almost gave out as she tried to stand. The officer took her arm, more for support than to restrain her. The two policemen that were to the left took up positions in front of them, the other two directly behind Sarina and the officer.

That was how Sarina was marched out of the San Destino International Airport terminal. They led her to a limousine parked between two police cars. The police officer opened the door for Sarina. She slid into the back-seat, and he got into the front passenger seat. The police car in front pulled out into the traffic. The town car followed, she guessed, with the other two officers in the police car behind them. Too shocked to feel embarrassment, she was cold and shaking. She knew she was in a lot of trouble.

How could those jewels Jason gave her to wear be part of the Crown Jewels? Her brain was racing. *Was he a jewel thief? He never wanted to tell me about his work. He drove that expensive sports car. Oh my God! What am I going to do?*

She had to protect herself, but she couldn't just sell Jason out. If he got arrested and sent to prison, she would never forgive herself. Inadvertently, it would be her fault. She was the one who had sold the jewels and brought attention to him.

The three cars were driving to the royal palace, up the winding road, passing the spot where Jason had found her. An image of the first kiss they had shared as he protected her from Chad flashed before her eyes. She saw him carrying her to his car and all that transpired from that point on to this.

The road widened, and they came to huge black-and-gold, intricately designed, wrought-iron gates. The car stopped, and the sentry peered into the driver's side, saluting the police officer. Then the sentry clicked a button on a handheld device, and the gates opened. Sarina dreaded every minute that passed. She pressed her knees together to keep them from shaking. The knot in her stomach tightened. They drove on up the road. She didn't notice the beautiful gardens on both sides of the drive. All at once, a magnificent white stone structure loomed in front of her. She knew from the little research she had done that the Royal Standard flying above the highest tower meant the king was in residence. She felt nauseous and lightheaded.

The car came to a stop at the main portico. Two guards stood at the entrance. The officer in the front seat came and opened the door for Sarina. Now, in the same manner as she'd been escorted from the airport, they marched her through a courtyard. She was grateful that they didn't have her in handcuffs, although nothing could be more humiliating than this.

Sarina entered the palace, overwhelmed by the grandeur. The ceiling was painted to look like the sky. Crystal chandeliers hung down the center above a white marble floor. A red-carpet runner ran down the center, corded off by gold ropes on either side. The walls had frescos depicting many different scenes, some of battles and some of women and children in gardens.

They turned down another corridor with a similar marble floor and more chandeliers lining the ceiling. Her tread slowed at the intimidating scene directly in front of her. Two uniformed guards stood at attention on either side of enormous carved-mahogany double doors, crystal sconces on either side of the entrance. Each guard reached for a knob and opened the doors for her to enter.

Sarina's feet sunk in the thick, cerulean-blue carpet. This room was spectacular, grander than the Oval Office. The enormous desk was decorated with intricate carvings of battle scenes on the front and side panels. The top was wood and dark leather. Two chairs faced the desk, both in a deep, rich burgundy trimmed in gold.

The guard said, "Please sit down, Madame."

She chose the seat closest to her, having lost the strength to walk any further. She watched as the guard placed her passport, boarding pass, and euros she'd had on the desk.

"Wait here. His Majesty will be with you shortly." The guard turned and left the room, closing the door behind him.

She sat with her head held high, her back straight and her hands folded on her lap, the knuckles white. Her shoulders ached. She was too worried to move.

Sarina had researched some of the places she would visit with Mrs. Williamson as her companion. She didn't have internet at home, another luxury they couldn't afford, so she went to the public library to use the internet. She knew that San Destino had a Ruling Family. The king did rule and wasn't just a figurehead, as in so many other European countries. He wasn't married and known as the Playboy King; she didn't know too much more. There were no photos of the family in the article that she'd read.

Sarina looked at a large oil painting hanging on the wall above the desk. The beautiful woman in the portrait wore a green velvet gown, and the diamond tiara on her head included five enormous emeralds. Her black hair curled about her shoulders. She had a flawless olive complexion, her blue eyes sparkling in a heart-shaped face with perfect brows. Admiring the painting, Sarina hesitated, then took a quick intake of breath as realization dawned. The woman in the painting wore a diamond-and-emerald pendant with matching earrings.

"Oh!" Her voice was barely a whisper, her eyes rounded, as she recognized them. She swayed in her seat, almost fainting. They were the ones she had sold. *Oh no, what will the king do with me? Prison for sure, but for how long? Forever?*

She thought of her mother and her sister. How would they get by? Her heart sank. As she held back tears, her throat felt as if she had eaten a bucket of sand. She couldn't even swallow. The knot in her stomach grew tighter and tighter. She couldn't think past breathing in and out. *I'm in so much trouble. I've never even gotten a parking ticket.* She was mortified by what she'd done.

Both doors opened. Sarina sat straight and tall, closed her eyes, and took a deep breath. She turned her head. Jason, dressed impeccably as this morning, entered.

She stood. "Oh! Oh no, Jason! They've arrested you, too! I had already made up my mind that I wouldn't tell them anything about you. I wouldn't tell them where I got the jewelry, no matter what they did to me. Because of my actions, you were found out. This is why you didn't tell me about your job. You're a jewel thief!"

His eyebrows shot up. For a moment, he looked at her, his long fingers curled around her upper arms, then he helped her to sit again. Calmly, he walked around the desk, pulled out the high-back chair with a crown emblazoned into the leather, and sat.

Sarina blinked, when she spoke, her voice was shrill. "What are you doing? Don't you know the trouble we're in?"

Jason sat back and looked at her. The anger in the depths of his blue eyes couldn't be mistaken. "There is only one thief here... Do you know who that is?"

She looked at him and shook her head.

His voice boomed, "It is you!" The fury in his deep voice made her tremble.

Sarina slowly looked at Jason, her lips parted in surprise. Jason sat at the king's desk. And she was the only thief here? The room spun as if she were on an out-of-control merry-go-round. Her chest tightened, and she fought to take in a breath. All at once, her body was icy cold. She trembled uncontrollably, and for the first time in her life, Sarina fainted.

~

HE SAW the color drain from her face as her body swayed. Jason couldn't get around his desk before she fell to the floor, the thick carpet somewhat cushioning the fall. He bent down to lift her and carried her to the burgundy couch. Sarina's breathing was shallow, and she was as pale as parchment. Jason was somewhat mollified when she'd fainted.

The unmitigated gall of her to steal from him, to sell his gift. He couldn't believe the phone call he received earlier today from his secretary. "Your Majesty, there's a jeweler on the line, and he'll only speak directly with you."

"I have the favorite emeralds that belonged to your late mother, Her Majesty Queen Rafaella."

"Impossible! Can you describe for me who brought them in?"

"Yes, yes, a young red-haired woman with green eyes."

Jason was amazed. "Thank you. Please bring them to the palace. You'll be greatly rewarded. Do you happen to know where she was going?"

"Yes, Your Majesty, she took a taxi to the airport."

"I ask you to never mention this to anyone."

"Oh no, Your Majesty, I won't speak of it ever."

Jason hung up the phone. He called the head of his

personal guard to have Sarina Moore detained and brought to his office. Then he told his secretary to cancel the rest of his appointments. He went to his private apartment in the palace, poured himself a whiskey, and waited.

She stirred. Jason poured a small amount of whiskey into a crystal glass. He helped her to sit up, handing her the glass with the amber liquid.

"Here, drink this. It may help you." He remained standing by the couch, unable to control his fury.

The trembling had begun again. She held the glass in both of her hands. Sarina took a sip and visibly shuddered. Some color returned to her cheeks, and the trembling lessened.

She looked up at him. "King Filippo, and not Jason Donato? I… don't understand… You're the king?"

There was ice in his voice. He looked down at her. "Filippo is one of my names, but you may continue to call me Jason. To answer your question—yes."

"I am deeply sorry about the jewelry. Believe me, all I ever wanted was to help my family. Please don't send me to jail. I didn't… know who… you were. I had no idea." Tears shimmered in her eyes before she took another sip of the whiskey.

Jason stood there, looking at Sarina. Why indeed did he give her those jewels? They matched her eyes. She looked beautiful in them. What made him give them to her? He wouldn't delve too deeply into any of that right now. As for using the name Jason Donato, that was a precaution he'd always taken, using that name so that no one would know who he really was. But not since college and graduate school.

He looked at her sitting on the couch. Her hand trembled as she held the glass, her head bowed. Somehow, he felt that he would never send her home; she was his. He found her; he took care of her. Jason wanted her until he tired of her. She was more than he ever dreamed a woman could be. He couldn't let her go. She belonged to him now.

Just like that, he was hard—fully aroused. All he wanted was to take her to bed. Her wild abandon was something that couldn't be faked. He'd introduced her to passion, and she was his now for as long as he wanted.

From that first intense kiss, he'd never hungered for a woman the way he did for her. She made him feel things he didn't want to think about. She got under his skin. Sex with Sarina was better than it had been in a long time. Better than with anyone else. He was a grown man, the ruler of a country, and these cravings that she made him feel... Maybe because she had been innocent, and he felt some responsibility for that, but even when he thought she was selling herself, he still had wanted her. Why indeed?

Women came easily to him, especially when they knew who he was. He was always careful, safe sex. The women he took to bed were discreet and knew beforehand what the rules were. Some fun and lots of sex. Jason wasn't averse to some kink if they were into it. He never got angry with them and certainly not the raging fury he felt when he learned that Sarina had left him. He was emotionally detached from his lovers. His heart never entered the picture. That was the way he liked it. The women knew that. Just sex. No long-term affairs and no commitments.

The longest any of these relationships lasted was three months. Then he'd get bored with them and move on. The women knew they would be well compensated with jewelry, but nothing ever from the Crown Jewels. He would buy them clothing, jewelry, some even an apartment, like his last lover, but never more than that. It was just sex for him, always had been and always would be, just sex.

He never brought any of them to San Destino. He took them to his London or Paris apartments. In Rome, he had a villa where he would go. When there were state affairs, his sister, who he had decreed the Crown Princess. Her Royal

Highness Princess, Catarina, was hostess. She and his brother-in-law Henri were his family, and he kept that part of his life separate. He didn't worry about heirs. Cat and her children would inherit.

Jason was in a raging temper, trying to sort out his own emotions. All he wanted to do was bury himself deep inside that redheaded witch and hope that she could make him forget his anger. He thought he would never see her again. When he got the call from the head of his personal guard that she was found and in their custody, he relaxed a little. All he wanted was her under him, naked and begging for that part of him that was now rock hard. He wanted to bury himself in her tight pussy and never stop making love to her.

Love! Love? Where did that come from? He forced that thought back deep into the recesses of his mind and focused on his anger.

He moved to the window and looked out at the Mediterranean and the Grand Marina in the distance. He had to get this rage under control. No one had ever dared to push him like she did. He turned to look at Sarina and made up his mind.

"Come with me."

HE LOOKED INTIMIDATING, with his face terse. She could see the fury burning in his blue eyes.

"You're lucky the jeweler you went to was very discreet and had the good sense to call me. We're the only ones who know of your deceit, of what you did, little thief."

"What are you going to do with me?" She couldn't help herself. She had to ask.

He raised one black brow.

One word came to mind. Jail. How would she stand it?

She hadn't even come to terms with the fact that she loved him. He hated her now. She saw it in the ice-cold brittle blue of his eyes. The warmth was gone.

She was nothing to him, and now he would send her to jail and, cliché or not, throw away the key. How would she stand being detained in his country, hearing about him? Hearing about him with someone else would kill her. Thinking of him making love with another woman—she felt physically sick. Dying inside, her heart ached. She knew there would be women. How could there not be? Her chest constricted, her heart breaking. Thinking of him making love to someone else sent pain knifing through her body.

"Is there anything I can say? You must understand my need to get home. I have responsibilities not only for my mother and sister, but for my job. If I lose that, then I'll have nothing. I was going to send you the money. I didn't know the sentimental value. Why did you give them to me? Why?"

Her voice rose in her own anger. "Why didn't you tell me who you are? I asked enough times. You didn't even use your real name. I guess it was a good joke for you to trick the stupid American girl. Take her to bed, use her, and then send her home. She would never know. That's why all the secluded locations—you didn't want to be seen with me."

Her throat clogged with tears. She wouldn't cry, not in front of him, never. It was bad enough that she had fainted. There was so much to think about—his deceit not using his real name, not telling her who he was. Oh, that was the worst. His deception, especially when she said that she would see about a job at the palace, oh, how he must have been laughing at her. She was getting angry again, she who hardly ever got upset. Sarina didn't think it was a good idea to get irritated with him right now. After all, he held her future— jail or home—in his hands. Her emotions were raw.

Sarina was startled out of her own thoughts, and at his

words, her bravado vanished. She stood on shaky legs. "Please, Jason, please don't send me to jail." Her voice was full of unshed tears.

"When I finish with you, you may wish for jail." His voice was harsh.

Her passport, the money she had gotten for the jewels, as well as the boarding pass were all left on his desk. She stood tall, all five feet three inches of her, shaking on the inside, her mouth dry. He opened a side door, took her by the wrist, and walked down a blue-carpeted hall.

Did all palaces have dungeons? Would she be allowed to call her mother? Her mother—a sadness came over her. Oh, how would she explain this?

They continued walking and came to an iron-scrolled door that led to a very secluded part of the garden. Arbors covered with hanging vines and climbing rose bushes with pink and white roses all hugged the stone wall. At the end of the walkway was a wrought-iron door in the arch of the wall. She could see more of the garden. He opened the door and led her up a large, open-air path of marble steps that hugged the stone wall of the palace. On the other side were arched openings with carved columns overlooking the garden below. Along the walkway, there were statues and more potted plants and the sparkling Mediterranean in the distance. Up, up, up they went.

*Weren't dungeons usually down and underground?* "Where are you taking me?" She tried to keep her voice steady, calm. But she failed.

"To your jail cell."

She swayed and worried she might faint again.

He looked at her.

She lifted her chin, held her head high, and looked directly in front of her. Taking deep, calming breaths, she walked next to him. The next door they came to wasn't as ornate. It was simple and made of wood, but it had letters on it. Just two letters: HM.

His Majesty? Where was he taking her?

Jason opened the door and stepped into the entry foyer. Sarina saw a large, ornate room with leather sofas facing each other, a coffee table between them, a fireplace, and two comfortable-looking chairs. Another room led to what appeared to be a dining room. He continued to walk, never letting go of her wrist, and came to white double doors trimmed in gold. He opened the doors and stepped aside.

Sarina saw a four-poster bed with his Royal Seal carved into a massive headboard. The bed was larger than any she had ever seen. It was covered with a deep-blue velvet coverlet that matched the drapes on the windows. The pillows were all in shades of blue with gold trim. High above the bed, jutting out from the wall, was a crown of gold, and deep-blue velvet drapes were swagged from both sides, cascading to the marble floor.

It was the most magnificent room she had ever seen, anywhere—magazines, TV, the world of the famously rich. Nothing came close to this room. She stopped short. Not moving, he tugged her into the room.

Sarina looked at Jason, her brows drawn together. He closed the doors. The click of the lock sent a chill racing up her spine.

# CHAPTER 7

The king's bedroom.

He didn't waste any time. "Get out of those clothes." His voice was full of suppressed anger.

"Please, Jason."

He stood there, handsome, broad shoulders, his muscular arms... His powerful hands with those long fingers were on his hips, and he waited.

*What? I thought he was taking me to jail, no trial, just convicted.* "Jason, I don't understand."

"What is it you do not understand? I said get out of those clothes."

She stood there staring at him, her brows furrowed... her lips parted to speak—

His low, ominous voice sent a shiver up her spine as he said, "Would you rather I rip them off your deceitful, thieving body?"

She looked at him. Her eyes widened as he took a step toward her. She stepped back, and he took another step. She stamped her foot and whirled around, taking some yoga breaths in a futile effort to calm her racing heart. She couldn't look at him... more calming breaths... Her trembling fingers reached for a pearl button at her throat.

"No," he thundered. "Turn around. I want to see what I'm paying for."

His deep voice vibrated through Sarina's body.

She closed her eyes... taking a deep breath. "Jason. Please."

He growled, and in two strides, he towered over her. Taking her blouse in his powerful fists, he ripped the delicate fabric, buttons flying in all directions.

"Ohhh!" She couldn't believe what he did. The sound of his deep growl was followed by the rasp of the zipper as he unzipped her slacks and yanked them along with her lace panties down over her hips. They fell to her feet. He unclasped her bra with the same vengeance. She stood before him naked and humiliated, tears stinging her eyes, her throat tight, her cheeks flaming with a furious blush. She covered her breasts and the juncture between her legs.

"Don't." His voice was low and menacing. "Put your hands at your sides," he ground out between clenched teeth.

With downcast eyes and a flaming face, she dropped her hands.

"Lie down on that bed. Make yourself ready for me."

Standing naked before him, her voice trembled. "Jason... not this way, not like this."

"Get on that bed." He pointed and raised his voice. "Now!" He thundered that last command.

She jumped and scrambled to do as he ordered. She bit her bottom lip. *I won't let him see me cower. I deserve this; I stole from him... Even now, I want him.*

～

Jason whipped off his jacket, looking at her as he worked to get his raging temper under control. He ripped his own shirt in his attempt to unbutton it. The only sound was the ping of the buttons as they scattered on the floor, joining hers. He didn't bother to take off his shirt. He grabbed his belt, unbuckled it, pulling the leather through the loops of his trousers, and tossed it to the marble floor. *Clang!* The buckle hit the floor at the same moment he kicked off his shoes. He kept his pants on, took his socks off, and threw them into a corner.

His jaw clenched. It felt as if it would break. Never had he experienced such a wave of raging anger and certainly not directed at a woman. Ice usually flowed through his veins where women were concerned. This one drove him to the brink, his temper flaring. His blood boiled.

When he found her gone, there were no words to describe the feelings that went through him. He had to have her. He needed nothing, no one... Yet he had to have this mere slip of a girl.

She'd been innocent... pure. She didn't realize who he was until he'd sat at his desk.

Sarina lay on his bed stiff, her eyes tightly closed. He cleared his mind and lifted his knee onto the mattress. Leaning over her seductive, naked body, he lifted her to him. She opened her emerald-green eyes. Jason took her lips with his in a possessive kiss. Forcing her soft lips apart, he thrust his tongue into her mouth as he probed, demanding a response.

His hands slid down the curves of her satin-smooth body. Lust burned in his brain. Never had he been so crazed over a woman. The sight of her naked curves inflamed him. He cupped a breast in one hand as his other moved around her back, arching her torso into him. Holding her breast, his fingers teased the nipple before his thumb rasped against the stiff peak.

His mouth moved down her neck. He felt her pulse pound under his lips as he traced the contours of her throat along her collarbone to lick the hollow, sliding his open mouth over her heated skin, moving down to her other lush, quivering breast. He circled that sweet flesh, and the nipple tightened to pebble hardness. Flicking the bud with the tip of his tongue, sucking and licking the texture of her skin, drinking in her taste.

SARINA TRIED to remain detached as his devilish tongue played with her breast. When he moved to her other breast… she knew she was failing miserably.

Jason slid up her body, returning to her mouth, kissing her as he spread her legs with his knee. Moving to her neck, he kissed a path of fire down between the valley of her breasts to her abdomen. Ever so slowly, he ran his hands up her inner thighs, his fingers gliding along her overheated skin. His thumbs on either side of her seam, massaging, teasing her, always stopping just before he reached the center of her desire.

He ran his hands down her inner thighs and back up again, avoiding what she needed. His hands at her breasts teased the nipples, his mouth closed over one nipple, and his fingers played with the other. Her breath came in short pants. He blew warm air over her wet nipple, making her gasp. She no longer cared. She squirmed under his hard body, heat coiling through her. She wanted to beg him to remove his pants and make love to her. She reached her arms around his neck, cupping his head, needing his kisses.

"Beg me," his deep, sexy voice whispered.

She groaned. The heat of his breath first on her nipple was now in her ear. He touched the lobe with the tip of his tongue, and her core throbbed for him.

Oh no! Exactly what she wanted to do. She tried to calm herself, dropping her hands as she blinked. Shaking her head, one word escaped her lips. "No," came out as a croak.

Ice-blue eyes looked at her, and he smirked. "You will."

Jason kissed her, his lips demanding a response. Seconds, minutes. His lips moved on her, sucking her bottom lip into his mouth. *God, I love that.*

Then he began his slow and torturous glide down the column of her neck, returning to a breast, flicking his tongue on the tight, erect nipple, sucking it into his mouth, circling his tongue over and over. His other hand slid to her other breast. With gentle pressure and a firm hand, his long fingers plucked her nipple.

She almost moaned but caught herself as he kissed the skin between the valley of her breasts and up the slope to her nipple, taking it into his oh-so-hot mouth.

She felt the heat of his hand spread as it moved down to her waist, sliding down past her navel. Her breath caught. If that wasn't enough, Jason ran his tongue down her body. Slowly, he blew his hot breath on her naked flesh, and goosebumps spread across her belly.

She groaned.

Sarina was on fire. With a will she didn't know she possessed, she stopped her body from moving and kept her hips still, no matter how much she wanted to beckon and encourage him. Her legs trembled with her effort. Sarina caught the moan that almost escaped her throat.

She was so hot, she thought she would die. His mouth, with that devil's tongue, knew all her secret places and what she loved—what he taught her to crave.

He rubbed her hot, feminine mound, and she held her

breath, waiting for what he would do next. His big hand cupped that same sensitive area, spread her legs. He moved down on the bed. His finger ever so slightly hovered above her crease, almost but not quite where she needed him to touch her. She held her breath, hoping he would send her soaring over the edge.

Ice-blue eyes stared up at her. She looked back at him. How many times had he done what she needed now? His finger was so close to where she needed him. Her heart pounded wildly, her breath hitching. The liquid fire in her needed to be quenched by him, only him, always him, by what he could give her.

She bit a corner of her bottom lip. On a ragged breath, her hips rose. She couldn't keep them still. Hot and desperate, her pelvis curled, showing him what she wanted, needed from him. Her body ached, her center on fire for him.

Once again, Jason said, "Beg me."

For a moment, her lids slowly slid over her eyes. A half moan, half groan escaped her. Then, without any shame, only need, Sarina looked into the blue depths and said, "Please, Jason, please make love to me."

He spread her then, and with the tip of his tongue, he circled her throbbing clit, then buried his tongue deep into her core, licking and thrusting so deep, curling his tongue up to her g-spot and back out to suck her clit once more. She climaxed in a rush of hot waves. He kept his mouth at her center, lashing her clit and outer lips. When she calmed, he did it all again, making her reach that fever pitch. He sucked at her clit, licked the walls of her vagina until she screamed in her pleasure, her hips rose, and her buttocks came off the bed, holding herself to his mouth.

She cried out, oblivious to everything but the ecstasy he gave her. Jason kept his mouth on her until the pulsing spasms stopped and her fingers relaxed in his hair. Through half-closed eyes, she gazed up at him. Her thighs rested on his shoulders. He kissed her center once more before he stood.

He peeled off his shirt and unzipped his pants, pushing them down his lean hips and over his muscle-covered legs. His huge erection seeped pre-cum. "Never mistake this for love. This is sex. Just sex, not love," he said in his deep voice.

Before his harsh words registered in her passion-filled brain, he spread her legs. If she expected roughness because of his anger and his hurtful words, it didn't come. He was as gentle with his entry as always. With his first thrust, amazingly, she was ready again. She wanted his velvety hardness going deep into her body. There was nothing she could do. She couldn't deny the desire she felt for him. The words hurt, but this was Jason, whom she loved and had stolen from. She knew she had hurt him as well.

HOW WAS it possible she would leave him? When he got the phone call and knew she was running from him, he went a little crazy, not like him at all. Women were always for his pleasure. It was different with Sarina. Her orgasms gave him the greatest sensual pleasure he had ever experienced, making his orgasms better than ever before.

Jason saw her face and how his words had hurt her. He never wanted to see that pain in her eyes again. He pushed further thoughts of this kind deep down in his mind. She would just have to resign herself to his wishes.

She was so worried when he walked into his office and thought he was also arrested. The satisfaction came when he saw the look on her face after she realized who he was. When she had fainted, he was concerned that he'd pushed her too far, though it did take the edge off his anger.

For the first time in his sexual life, Jason forgot to use a condom. She had aroused him and blinded him to all, except being inside her tight sheath. Her hot, wet heat surrounded him. Her mewling and the longer, deeper moans drove him higher than he had ever been before. She was the most passionate woman he'd ever known; she held nothing back, lifting her hips to meet his thrusts.

She climaxed again, her honey-hot pussy clenching and unclenching around him, drawing him in, stroking him. It took all his concentration to hold back. Jason got his passion under control. He would prove to her that she needed this, needed him. He brought her to that frenzied point again. When she whimpered, he held her buttocks in his hands, massaging the satin flesh, and buried himself as deep as he could. His balls tightened, and heat spread up his spine. He couldn't hold back any longer, groaning as he shot his passion into her. No woman had ever felt so good, so hot, so tight, so perfect.

Jason kept most of his weight off her, buried deep in Sarina. They were both breathing heavily. Gradually, as their breathing returned to normal, he brushed her hair from her flushed face and held her, not wanting to let go. Savoring the moment, he wanted it to never end. *So not like me at all.*

Sarina sighed, her legs around his waist, ankles locked behind his back. She looked euphoric. She lifted her hands to his face and traced his cheekbones with her fingertips. Then she brushed her lips along his jaw, running the tip of her pointing finger over his lower lip. She sighed, "Mmm." Capturing his lips, her tongue slid in his mouth, and swirled around his.

He groaned. "You think you can kiss me like that without any consequences?" He growled, "I'm not made of stone."

Her lazy, dreamy smile sizzled through him.

Her lids closed over her emerald-green eyes. "You feel like solid steel covered in velvet."

"Kiss me again, beautiful."

She did, and he thrust his hips forward, in and out, with strong, deep, sure strokes. He rose, guiding her legs over his shoulders. He thrust to the hilt, holding her buttocks, lifting her to his deep penetration.

"Open your eyes. Look at me, Sarina," he breathed. So hot, so sweet, her contractions drove him. He thrust into the scalding heat of her.

"You're mine. Mine for as long as I want you."

She writhed against him, moaning her pleasure.

"Say it. Tell me." He thrust deeper, grinding his hips into her.

"Yes, Jason. Yes… yesss." Her fingernails dug into his biceps.

Their bodies fused, he held her to him.

"Now, ahh, ahh, Jason, I'm coming." Her inner core contracted around him.

Jason pistoned harder, faster, pumping in and out of her wet heat, propelling himself toward his own powerful orgasm. Gasping, he emptied himself, filling Sarina to over-flowing. For the second time, he forgot a condom. Her silky-smooth legs slid from his shoulders.

Jason rolled over, taking Sarina with him to lie on top of him. He smoothed her mass of red hair from her flushed face. She rested her head on his shoulder, and her soft lips kissed his neck.

Holding her curves to his sated body, Sarina fell asleep in the circle of his arms.

*What am I going to do with her?* He wanted her; he wanted this always. He breathed in her fragrance, mixed with the scent of sex, and he fell asleep.

Hours later, Sarina moved in his arms.

"Hungry?" he asked, burying his nose in her hair.

"Yes, actually, I'm starving."

"Steak or seafood, maybe salmon?"

"Mmm, I think steak… for strength."

He rolled over, picked up the phone on the bedside table, and ordered dinner to be set up on the terrace.

"We'll have time for a shower before we eat." He took her hand, twining his fingers with her smaller ones, and they padded into the bathing suite. The sunken tub was filled, and the water swirled through the jets. He bypassed the tub and went to the shower. He turned on the steam, and the large enclosure filled with billowing clouds. Lifting Sarina into his arms, he carried her into the shower. Her silky arms looped around his neck, and she rested her head on his shoulder while he walked to the marble bench that ran along the far wall. Jason sat on the bench, holding her in his lap. He kissed her temple, smoothing her hair back.

"This is so relaxing," she said as she snuggled into his arms.

After a while, he turned on the rain shower. Reaching for the bar of soap, he rubbed his hands together, making a thick lather, and soaped her breasts. When her nipples tightened, he stood her next to him, turning her so he could lather her back and buttocks.

"Let me," she said as she picked up the bar of soap. The suds sliding down her body.

He stood, looking at her, searching the emerald-green depths. Gradually, a smile played around his lips, and spreading his arms out, he said, "I'm all yours."

SARINA NEVER DID MORE than touch his body. He'd always been the one to make her come with his mouth. She felt shy, but she was determined to do to him what he did to her. She reached up and soaped his broad shoulders, her soapy hands moving to his muscular chest. Eyes downcast, she wouldn't look at him. She soaped down his abdomen, her fingers slipping over each rock-hard muscle as she went on.

She almost lost her nerve as her soapy hands slid lower. She hesitated. He was huge and fully erect. Her hands skirted around down his thighs. Dropping to her knees, she soaped his legs, the rain shower rinsing the suds off him. With a boldness she didn't know she possessed, she touched the smooth, velvet tip of his erection with her tongue.

He closed his eyes, and, lifting his handsome face to the stream of water, he stroked her cheek. She pressed forward, opening her mouth.

He groaned. "Are you sure?"

She didn't answer, taking more of him into her mouth. Jason's fingers ran into her hair, and she reached to hold his shaft. Not sure exactly what to do, she adjusted to him in her mouth. Her tongue stroked him.

"Oh sweet, yes, like that."

She stroked his thigh, and he pressed his hips forward. She gazed up to see him looking at her. *I want to please him, love him.*

"You're beautiful. Keep doing that with your tongue." She did and felt a zing of heat between her legs. She moved forward as he pushed his hips forward. Her eyes rounded at the feel of him moving further into her mouth. She moaned and then slipped her hand up and around to his granite-hard butt. She took more of his long length into her mouth, wondering if her mouth could open as wide as he was.

He groaned. "You don't have to…" She held his gaze. *I want to.*

Jason cupped her head in his big hands and used small, quick movements, pushing in and out of her mouth. Sarina felt comfortable and wanted him to come like this. *How will it feel? I want this and want to please him so much.*

He groaned, and she felt the warmth of his ejaculation. Sarina instinctively swallowed. He held her head to him for a heartbeat, then lifting her to stand, he gently kissed her. "You are beautiful."

Sitting on the bench, he tugged her onto his lap. This time, she faced away from him, her back to his chest. He held an arm around her under her breasts.

Jason whispered into her ear, "Spread your legs over my thighs."

*Oh God, what is he going to do?* Slowly, she moved her legs.

He plucked a nipple. "I have you right where I want you."

She shivered with the water beating on them. He kissed her wet neck, then he spread his knees, opening her wider. He reached his fingers to part her, baring her clit. His other hand slid down her waist to her abdomen, gliding down and finding her opening. His finger rested at her vagina.

She squirmed on his lap, her wet hair plastered to her neck and shoulders, curling around her breasts, her nipple peeking between the strands of wet red hair. He sent his finger into her heat.

Sarina cried out, and her head rolled on his shoulder, quivering in his arms. She lifted an arm to hold his head, her fingers at the nape of his hair. She undulated on his lap, and her knees rose. Jason slipped a second finger into her core at the same instant his other hand rolled her clit between his thumb and finger.

She moaned at the zing of pleasure. Her knees inched higher, opening herself fully to his fingers. "Jason, oh Jason," she screamed as the waves of her climax radiated through her body. She lay sprawled across his lap, her spine pressed to his chest.

"More?" he breathed. His lips were against her neck, and

he pressed her clit, sending another wave of delicious shudders through her. *I love him.*

Sarina knew she loved him even before she tried to leave. Although his words were cruel and meant to hurt her, his actions were not. His gentleness proved that to her.

Again, she found herself without clothes, standing naked in the middle of the bathing suite. Jason handed her one of his shirts. He wore loose-fitting white linen pants with a blue-and-white, striped, short-sleeved shirt he left most of it unbuttoned.

"I like your bare skin, the gentle curves of your body, but I guess to have dinner, you should wear my shirt."

She slipped her arms into the silk fabric, and he helped her roll up the sleeves. "You could get my clothes for me," she snarked.

A ghost of a smile touched his lips as he shook his head. Taking her hand, they walked out to the terrace.

She hesitated for a second, barefoot, with only his shirt for modesty.

"They're gone and won't return until I call."

Sarina sat at the square table covered in a blue damask cloth. The table was set with china plates and crystal wine glasses. A floral arrangement of gardenias sat low in the center of the table. Squat, thick candles were lit and placed around the flowers. Next to his seat on a high stand was a sterling silver bucket and a bottle of champagne. The aroma of the food made Sarina realize how hungry she was. When he looked at her, she put her fork down, unable to meet his eyes.

Jason reached across the table and took her hand. He kissed the palm. Her gaze met deep blue eyes.

"Do you know how beautiful you are?"

She shook her head. "Not true."

"I have never met a woman more giving or more beautiful

than you. Eat… you're going to need your strength." Her eyes rounded in surprise. He'd remembered her earlier teasing remark. The fire in his blue eyes warmed her cheeks.

He poured the champagne. They sipped the sparkling wine under a blanket of stars; the moon hung low in the sky. They ate, and then he took her inside. The bed had been made with clean sheets, with the covers folded at the foot. Their clothes were gone from where they lay; even the buttons had been picked up.

She smirked. "You must have missed this kind of service while we were at the beach house."

"You think they didn't come to take care of me? My staff was never more than a phone call away, and the caretakers for the beach house," he shrugged one broad shoulder, "were always nearby, in their own home on the property. I made sure you never saw anyone but me."

Her head lifted, and her mouth dropped open, thinking of the times they had made love outside.

"Do not stress yourself. My staff is discreet, and only I have ever seen your lovely naked body or heard your screams of pleasure."

Heat shot into her cheeks, and she was unsure whether she felt better hearing that he protected their privacy.

"No clothes, just sex," he said and pulled her to him. "You're too sexy in my shirt." He kissed her brow.

"Well, then give me back my clothes," she said in a husky voice. He was so close, his erection pressing into her.

He chuckled and reached to pull his shirt over her head.

She gasped.

His lips brushed hers, and Sarina parted her lips to his exploration. Her arms wound around his neck, and he tumbled her onto the bed. Jason stroked a finger between her legs. "So wet and hot for me."

She sighed, pulling his head down to capture his lips. He

angled his mouth and slid his tongue into her mouth. Sarina sucked on his tongue. *I'll never forget his kisses, his taste. Ahhh, the way his thumb is sliding over my clit.*

Sarina parted her thighs and lifted her knees, opening herself to him. He thrust two long fingers into her, his thumb adding more pressure to her clit. Her moan turned into a scream that he muffled with his mouth.

She ran her fingers through his thick, black hair. "I need you in me." The words puffed out of her.

"Soon," he said. His blue eyes gazing at her, he inched down her body to her erect nipples, licking one…

"Oh, ohm," she moaned.

Jason moved down on the mattress, capturing her spread thighs between his broad shoulders. Her red hair was a mass of tangles on the pillow, breasts arching, her erect pink nipples wet from his mouth. He spread her, exposing the glistening pink flesh to his view. Her fingers reached for him.

He touched the tip of his tongue on the exposed nerves of her desire, pressing the side of her clit that he knew drove her crazy.

Her fingers massaged his head, pulling him closer, and he opened her wider to kiss her center. The flat of his tongue licked the tender folds, sinking into her. She quivered in his hands. Her green eyes filled with desire.

He lifted his head. "Put your feet on my shoulders."

She moaned, "Oh, God," before she rested her feet on his shoulders.

Jason slid a finger deep into her wet heat. He crooked his finger, rubbing the sensitive g-spot.

Her fingers tangled in his hair. "Oh yes, y-yesss," she cried, moving her fingers on his scalp in the same way he rubbed. "Yes… yes… yes. Oh, Jason."

Her vagina clenched and unclenched when the spasms slowed. He sucked her clit, starting another wave of shuddering bliss. Her feet slipped off his shoulders to the mattress, quivering, and she panted. Jason slid up her damp, sated body. He reached for a condom, rolled it on, and in one sure thrust, he buried himself in her heated core.

She held his head and snaked her tongue out to run along his lips. He throbbed, and she reached her hands down his back, massaging his spine, reaching his butt. Her lids slid over her eyes, and her smile melted his control. "Open your eyes, *cara mia.*" He thrust into her a handful of times.

"Oh, Jason… I—I lov—" Sarina buried her face in his neck before sprinkling kisses on his chest.

He couldn't hold back any longer. He gritted his teeth. "Come for me." Buried to the hilt, he pulsed in her heat. She stroked him on the waves of her orgasm to his own shuddering release. He rolled to his side, dragging her along to hold through the night and into the late morning.

Jason had their meal brought to the sitting room. She never saw anyone but him. He wanted every moment with her that he could have.

On the second evening, when she reached for his shirt, he gave her a green satin dressing gown. "Here, *cara*… for you, but only this and no more."

She slipped her arms into the green silk, pulling the fabric closed, and tied the sash.

"Even this clings too sexy on your curves."

He wore jeans and a loose-fitting shirt, she in the dressing gown. He led her to the terrace.

"Is that a violin I hear?"

"The musicians are in the garden below the terrace." He leaned close and whispered in her ear, "Completely out of sight."

He bowed low and put out his hand. "Dance with me."

She hesitated and shook her head. "I'm barefoot. Besides, I never learned how to waltz."

"Another first I'll have the pleasure of introducing you to," he said as he extended his hand for her to take.

She felt her cheeks flame as she took his hand. Then he wrapped his arms around her. His chin rested on the top of her head, and they swayed to the music. It was the most wonderful and romantic thing in the world to her: the music, Jason's scent—cologne and pure, virile man—his arms holding her. The night sky full of stars, the air held the fragrance from the gardens. He kissed her brow and lifted her into his arms. The music continued long after they had gone into the bedroom.

Jason kept her in his bed for three days. Sarina was torn. She loved him; of that she had no doubts. Yes, she had stolen from him, and he wouldn't send her to jail, though this may very well be worse. He said he would keep her until he was finished with her. She never wanted him to be done with her. She loved him, but she knew how helpless, hopeless the situation was. He was a king, not just any man.

He was on the terrace, dressed in casual clothes. Jason stopped pacing and went to sit on the chaise lounge. He sat pondering on the past three days. Perhaps his ancestors felt as if it was their right to keep captives. He knew they had. There were pirates in his lineage who plundered and took what they wanted... but this wasn't who he was. What had come over him? To keep her locked up with him and use sex to punish her—for what? Was it the selling of the jewels, or was it that she wanted to leave him?

When he got that phone call... he couldn't believe that she had the nerve to sell the jewelry he gave her. Though her determination showed Jason her strong character, the loyalty to her family was admirable. All he saw was that angel's face and lethal body, the combination—heaven on earth. He wouldn't let her go.

Sarina was in the shower, and Jason called for an outfit to

be brought to his apartment. A white eyelet sundress, along with a frilly lace bra and panties, lay across the bed. Sandals and a wide-brim hat had been placed on the chair next to the bed.

His cell phone rang. Glancing at the screen, he sighed and answered, "Hello, Catarina."

"Filippo, you have been home for three days, and I haven't seen you once. Now I hear that you've had a woman in your apartment! What's going on?"

*Sarina is my business.* "Cat, not now. I'll inform you in due time. As for now, don't ask me any questions. I'm returning to the beach house. I'll be back during the day when necessary to conduct any business that requires my attention."

He heard the concern in her voice. "I understand. Just as long as you're all right. Filippo—"

"No more questions." He pressed end, disconnecting the call more abruptly than he intended.

No one ever dared question him. He wouldn't tolerate this, especially not about Sarina. His sister would just have to let him alone. He wanted to keep Sarina all to himself. He wanted all her time for as long as he could.

The entire time she was at the palace, in Jason's bedroom, they didn't mention any of the circumstances that led up to her being taken from the airport. No serious conversations.

Jason looked out over the clear, blue water of the Mediterranean and thought back to a time when he was carefree and didn't hide his emotions or who he was. A time when he knew how he felt about his future and the responsibilities that would one day become his. His early education had been here on San Destino, then University in England, and graduate school in the US, at Yale. Funny that Sarina lived in Connecticut. She was a child when he studied for his MBA.

He had friends and acquaintances, but once it was learned

that he was the Crown Prince of San Destino, things always changed. Women chased him before, but when they learned he was a prince, they perked up, and he knew they no longer saw him, but the life they could have. He focused on his education, keeping his identity secret. The secrecy became so firmly ingrained in him, he carried it wherever he went. He had buried his feelings so far down into his soul, it was second nature to him now. He always kept himself separate from his emotions, so much so that he wasn't sure he could ever change. This was who he was and who he had become.

Jason was as old as Sarina was now when his parents had tragically died in a car accident. He thought back to that tragic day. Catarina had been away at boarding school in Switzerland. He had been home only three short months after receiving his MBA. His father wanted him to have a quiet year before gradually transitioning into his role and taking on more responsibilities.

That awful day, he was out sailing when a motorboat with men from the royal guard came up alongside his boat. Jason knew instantly that it wouldn't be good news. He knew all the guards by name. Joseph had boarded. "Your Royal Highness, I have terrible news. Their Majesties were in a car accident," Joseph himself, overcome with emotion, said. "They have perished along with the driver and one of their guards."

Jason was too shocked to instantly speak. His parents had been on tour in Spain. His mind was numb from the shock.

"Your Majesty, we'll take you to the palace."

"Yes, has my sister been informed?"

"No, we were waiting for you to let us know how you wished us to proceed with Her Royal Highness Princess Catarina."

Jason had climbed into the speedboat and was whisked to shore and to the palace. In the car, he'd gathered his thoughts. He had to tell Catarina himself. "Call her school and be sure that you explain to the headmistress that absolutely no one is to say anything to Catarina before I arrive. Let us see if we can get the media's cooperation to allow us some privacy while we lay my parents to rest. I want to fly to Switzerland immediately and bring Cat home." On the flight, he'd changed into a suit, learned more of the tragedy, and made the necessary arrangements to bring home the bodies of his parents.

Though there was a ten-year gap in their ages, he and Cat had always been close. The headmistress had left him to use her office, and Catarina was brought in. When she saw Jason, she ran into his arms. He'd held her and told her the devastating news. He held her while she cried out her sorrow.

Jason had to take on the responsibility of his sister's welfare as well as the country that they loved. As time passed, Catarina had grown into a beautiful young woman, more and more like their mother.

As the years went by, Jason grew more cynical in his feelings toward the opposite sex. He was convinced that he didn't need love. He kept his heart safe from pain by locking it away where no one could get to it.

Love was for other people. Catarina had found the love of her life with Henri. As for him, he enjoyed having sex. No attachments other than the mutual enjoyment sex brought him and his partner of the moment. He liked tall blondes, brunettes—models, actresses, other royals. He became known as the Playboy King. It was an undesirable distinction, but one the media liked to use. No one would dare say that to his face. He'd been content with his life the way it was —at least that was how he'd felt—until Sarina came along.

SARINA WALKED out onto the terrace. The view was spectacular, with the Mediterranean glittering like diamonds in the distance. The air was perfumed from the garden below; terracotta pots with blooming flowers were scattered along the stone floor, and urns filled with more flowers sat along the balcony. The best view of all was Jason. Adonis come to life, jet-black hair and his blue eyes that made the sky pale in comparison dressed in slacks that hugged long, muscular legs. The navy-blue polo shirt he wore stretched across broad shoulders, defining his pecs and hinting at his washboard abs.

Sadly, now she knew he could never marry her. He was a king after all, and she… a nobody, from a small town in Connecticut. Cinderella was a fairytale that she read to her kindergarten class. It was just that, a fairytale. There would be no happily ever after for her. She would always remember him. How could she not? She knew there would never be anyone else.

Her heart snagged. All she would ever have to hold her were these memories of the man she loved. The ache in the center of her chest grew. The only time she didn't feel this terrible pain was when he was making love to her. She'd caught herself more than once, almost saying she loved him.

Jason had to let her go home now! Her heart was already shattered. If she stayed any longer, she feared she would throw herself at his feet and beg him to keep her as his mistress or in whatever capacity he wanted. She would settle for whatever he offered to be with him.

He rose from the chaise. "You found my gift. Sit with me so we can have breakfast."

"I'll pour the coffee for us." Sarina poured two cups of coffee from the pot on the trolley. She put some fruit, cheese, and a roll on a china plate. Sarina served him and then made a similar dish for herself. She had no appetite—only a hollow ache in the pit of her stomach. She sat at the table under an umbrella. Jason moved forward, taking her hands in his.

*Oh dear, this won't be good.* She couldn't think clearly when he touched her. She always ended up giving in to him.

"I want us to go back to the beach house."

Of all the things Sarina thought he would say, that wasn't one of them. "Jason, this is crazy. I have to go home, now more than ever."

"All in good time. My car is parked on the drive."

She sighed and nodded. His brilliant smile took her breath away, then he stood and led her out to his car. He opened the passenger door for her to slip into his red Ferrari. As he drove off the palace grounds, she didn't look back. She couldn't and didn't want to think of whom Jason was. She looked directly ahead.

# CHAPTER 8

The mansion on the beach looked golden, bathed in morning sunlight. Jason drove his red Ferrari up the circular drive. Sarina on the seat next to him. Her breath caught as she thought, *He is so handsome.* She sighed, wanting to soak up as many memories of him and their time together to keep close to her heart; they would have to last her a lifetime. She would never get over him.

He drove around the fountain, turned off the engine, and came around the car to open her door. Jason held her hand as he led her around the side of the house. They walked down the stone pathway, past the infinity pool, down to the beach. Climbing vines of roses, gardenia bushes, and jasmine lined the path. An arbor of bougainvillea in pinks and purples arched across the path to stroll under on the way to the secluded beach. The sandy shore spread out before them like a carpet.

She stopped to slip off her shoes, then twined her fingers with his longer ones. They walked in silence to the water's edge. The sand felt cool on her feet, as Jason's nearness heated her more than the sun ever could. He stood behind her as they faced the water, slipping his arms around her waist. She leaned back into his powerful chest. His strong, lean body pressed into her.

His lips touched her ear, murmuring silky smooth, "I would like you to stay for the rest of the summer."

She tensed at his words, and his arms tightened around her waist, coaxing her to relax as he kissed her temple.

"There are so many feelings and emotions we need to explore." Another kiss before he continued, "When the summer is over, you can go home if that's what you want. You know I always intended to pay for your airfare."

He kissed behind her ear and down her neck. "I'll give you the money you were expecting to earn from the Williamsons."

She moved away from his lips, frowning, and half-turned in his arms, tilting her head up to look at him. Her eyes rounded, and her stiff fingers reached for his forearms, tugging to get out of his embrace. He released his hold, as she spun to face him.

*He's going to treat me like a prostitute? The same way Joanna Williamson thought I'd sell myself.* Every kiss, every touch, all their lovemaking suddenly felt cheap. She felt cheap and dirty. Why did he think he had the right to do this to her? *You gave him the right,* her brain screamed.

His touch… was enough to drive her over the edge. She lost all her will, always melting in his arms. She was too weak around him. Her resolve had always crumbled, astounded at how easily she kept falling into his bed. Sarina couldn't talk, unable to say anything at all. There was no way she could spend any more time with him and keep her heart safe, keep her dignity. This wasn't a relationship that would lead to anything other than a broken heart for her. Who was she kidding? Her heart was broken.

He was used to women taking from him. Jason had to recognize that she wasn't one of them. He couldn't buy her. Now that she realized who he was—the Playboy King—eventually, the paparazzi would get this into the papers. Her mother, and her sister. What would they think?

Her heart! She had to protect her heart.

Heat rose into her cheeks, her eyes flashing her anger at him. Sarina's voice rising with each word. "I want to go home now. You must let me go. I won't take your money!" She took a breath and somewhat calmed. "The airfare is a loan that I'll pay back." She shook her head. "I won't take anything from you."

He raised a black brow at her.

She felt the heat radiate in her cheeks, remembering the jewels. "I won't let you demean what we had. You and I both know I can't stay any longer. I must get home. You're a king, for goodness sake!"

"That's precisely why I kept my identity from you and not for the reasons you thought. I'm not ashamed of you. I didn't want to see you change, to put my title above me, the man."

She closed her eyes, then looked up at him. She blew out a breath in frustration. "Who you are makes you the person you are. I can't believe you don't see this. I can never be more to you than a summer romance—a fling. That's all this can ever be."

He shouted, "We're not children. I am aware of that." Scrubbing a hand through his hair, he added, "We need to explore the relationship we're developing. From the beginning, we have had an attraction. We must give this more time. See where it leads."

"It can't lead anywhere." There was a special connection between them, but she recognized that there wasn't any place for it to go. Staying with him would rip her apart. She knew nothing would come of this, no matter what Jason said. *How will I go on living without him?*

While she was at the airport, even before she realized who he was and how helpless the situation was, she knew she would never forget him. She knew from the beginning that he was domineering, and she didn't possess the power to resist. She never met anyone like him, nor would she ever again.

She'd dated briefly while at the university and, more recently, an attorney from a local law firm, but their kisses had done nothing. There was no excitement. Certainly, none of the heat that Jason brought out in her. He was the sexiest man she'd ever met.

JASON WATCHED the emotions pass over her beautiful, heart-shaped face and knew that his position in life made this difficult for her. *Good, you play with fire, you could get burned.* Determined at any cost to keep her with him through the summer, he knew how to persuade, and "no" wasn't a word he gave in to, certainly not from this siren of a woman.

He would show Sarina how much staying with him would benefit her. After all, women could be bought with jewels and clothes. No matter what she said, the money would help her and her family.

His previous lovers understood what a relationship with him meant. They were worldly and discreet. *But she isn't like the others. She was a virgin. Naive to the ways of money and power. Look what almost happened to her, at the hands of Joanna Williamson and Chad.* The more he thought of that, the angrier he became. He was determined to spend time with Sarina, keep her for as long as he wanted, then help with a nest egg for her future.

Jason slipped his arm around Sarina's tiny waist, bringing her closer to his side as they strolled along the sandy beach. "This place… has always been my sanctuary from the demands of my position. I would come here and let the sea relax me and clear my mind so that I could do what is best for San Destino and its people. My father and mother spent much time here, and when my sister and I were younger, we spent our summers here. We relaxed away from the palace and the demands that went along with it. My mother didn't have a title. She was Sicilian, born in Palermo."

He smiled at Sarina as the sea breeze ruffled her hair and the sun turned the red locks to copper. "She met my father while he was touring Italy. He fell instantly in love with her, and they married. She was happy here in San Destino, as queen. She embraced the people, helping my father. When we stayed here, she would cook some of our meals. My parents felt it was important to know how to provide for ourselves. This would help us better serve the people of San Destino."

Jason glanced down as Sarina bent to brush a piece of driftwood from their path. "My father and mother would take us out sailing almost every day. We would go horseback riding. We had minimal staff here. My father loved to drive through the countryside, mingle with the people, learn what they desired, needed. Sometimes, he would take me with him. During the summer, he would return to the palace to conduct any business that was required of him. Some of my happiest memories were here in this place."

Jason paused for a moment, looking out at the sea. He sighed, his voice soft. "After my father and mother died, it took me a long time to come back here. When my sister Catarina and her husband married, they came often, but for me, it was difficult. I remembered all the good times knowing they would never be again."

Sarina put her arm around his waist and rested her head on his chest. She gave him a squeeze but said nothing.

"I had just finished graduate school when my parents perished in an automobile accident. I threw myself into the work my father had begun to make San Destino prosper. I invoked the help of my ministers. We'd focus on economic independence." He hugged her to him as he spoke. "Cat continued with my mother's charities and some new ones that she was interested in to help our people. I traveled to other countries to bring tourism here. With the increase in tourists, we built more hotels, grander and exclusive hotels catering to the wealthy. The island has many natural resources that I wanted to promote. My people have prospered in many ways. The money the government brings in from tourism goes directly back to the people. Medical and education are free to every citizen of San Destino."

Jason glanced down at Sarina for a moment. "Prince Henri, Cat's husband, is a good man from an old and prominent European family. Together, we've worked to make San Destino the thriving nation it now is. Their three children are growing up to one day assume their duties."

He stopped walking; the waves lapped at the shore, the sand cool on his feet, as he glanced down at Sarina. Her beautiful face was sun-kissed, the green eyes vibrant, no longer angry.

"Do you know where I had been the evening I found you?"

She shook her head. "No, how could I?"

"That very day I had arrived home from Paris, where I told Claudia...my most recent mistress—"

Sarina looked up into his eyes.

"Don't look so shocked—I politely said to her that I would no longer see her. She wasn't distressed. She knew it meant a large gift of jewelry, as well as the deed to the apartment she lived in. No Crown Jewels for her."

He hugged Sarina to him as he said, "You, little thief, are the only one I've ever given those."

Sarina hung her head and missed the smile Jason gave her.

"Claudia was happy with our arrangement. She was going to keep the gifts of jewelry I had already given her... the clothes I bought for her." He smiled as he continued, "I didn't go empty handed. I brought a velvet box containing a sapphire-and-diamond necklace, earrings, and a bracelet. She was pleased with her gifts."

He sighed. Holding Sarina once again, he said, "Women are happy to receive gifts from me. They know it won't be long before they are replaced, so I cannot fault Claudia for taking what I gave her and preparing for her future. All my other lovers had known who I was. They all knew... that when the relationship was over, they would graciously accept the gifts I gave them, and I would be on my way."

He held her gaze. "I have sex, Sarina, only sex. Never more than that. Just sex, no strings, no commitments. None of the women were ever invited to San Destino."

SARINA WAS APPALLED by what he told her, but again, she had always believed the best in people. Why else would she believe Mrs. Williamson? To take money or gifts in exchange for sex amounted to selling herself. Sarina looked up into his handsome face. His blue eyes were gentle. He gave her a sheepish smile that made him look like a young boy. She had no words to let him see that there were people who didn't want money in exchange for friendship. His cynicism ran deep.

Her lids slid over her eyes for a brief second, and she felt her heart twist for him. *He must be so lonely... He doesn't even realize it.* They walked in silence, listening to the surf.

"I must tell you where I'd been the night I found you."

Her stomach clenched. She was certain she wouldn't like what he was about to tell her. She didn't say a word; she held her breath.

"Years ago, I had searched for a reputable builder to transform the Grand Marina and build the hotels I envisioned. I met Howard Williamson."

She stopped walking, and he glanced down at her. She gazed into his blue eyes.

Jason took her hand. "Let's sit here."

They sat on a patch of grass near the beach house, having circled back. Sarina sat and hugged her knees up into her chest. She rested her head on them.

"We met, and I hired him to build many of the hotels in San Destino. Howard's firm extended the Grand Marina and built the Yacht Club. My people are wealthy in their own right because of some of his architectural designs. Through the years... Howard and I have always kept in contact. I know he indulges his wife and how devoted she is to both Chad and Derrick. She spoils them."

Sarina huffed at that last remark. She didn't like where this conversation was heading.

"I've kept this from you for too long... I had been invited to the *Carmella* for dinner. At the end of the evening before I debarked, Joanna was notified that a female member of the crew went missing. Chad borrowed a car from the harbormaster, and he and Derrick went to search for the person.

"When you fell on the road, and you asked for my help, I realized who you were. I decided to give you my protection and keep you safe from them. I never expected... to find a passionate virgin. An innocent beauty who has turned my world upside down. The rest," he shrugged one broad shoulder, "is the reason we're here. You and I have unfinished business. We both know that."

Sarina shook her head and let him talk. She was too upset. Her lips thinned as she allowed the tension in her body to fuel her anger. *Now I'm unfinished business. He knew who I was from the very beginning? He thought I was a prostitute. Oh, king or not, his audacity is unbelievable.*

She sprang to her feet and pushed the hair from her face, dropping her hands to rest on her hips. "So, you pretended you knew nothing about me. How could you do that? I trusted you and relied on you." She was upset. Her head pounded. "I can't believe how you used me! You thought I was, I was a…"

*Calm down, you're stuttering.* "Did you think I was easy? Oh, how happy you must have been when without any effort at all on your part, I fell right into your bed! Oh, what a fool I am." Her hands opened and clenched. "Agrrrh."

She turned from him and stormed back to the house. He caught her and spun her around. Holding her upper arms, his grip, though gentle, restricted her movement.

"No! Don't touch me." She tried to break free of his grasp.

Jason dropped his hands. "Wait," he commanded.

"I want to go home. Now!" Mortified and feeling used, she had to get away. She wouldn't let him touch her. Each time he did, she ended up in his bed. She didn't trust herself to be strong. She was a pushover where he was concerned. His nearness always made her reason fly right out of her head. Just one touch, a look, and she melted into a puddle of need at his feet. She had to get away.

Jason ran long, lean fingers through his hair, scrubbing his scalp, his own frustration showing plainly on his face. "I'll send you home when I'm good and ready," he said in an autocratic tone, his demeanor despotic, looking down his nose at her.

Sarina's chest heaved against the white eyelet of her summer dress. Sparks of green fire shot out of her eyes, into his, cool and calm gaze.

"Agrrrh, fine. I can't reason with you—but I'm telling you this—I will not," she stamped her bare foot, "share your bed any longer." She spun around, red silken hair flying around her shoulders, curls bouncing, as she stormed into the house.

He found her in the hall, carrying a pile of her garments, still on their hangers, draped over her arm. She ignored him and stomped with a determined step to another bedroom away from his.

"What are you doing?" Jason demanded.

She stopped and looked at him over the clothes in her arms. "I won't share your bed any longer. I'll stay here until you send me home, simply because I have no choice, but not in your bed. I would rather find a job so I can make the money I need for my airfare."

"No," boomed out of him, and he clenched his teeth. He wouldn't shout.

She raised one perfectly arched, auburn brow at him and shook her head from side to side. "Stubborn, and oh so demanding," she said and walked past him into the bedroom, flinging the clothes onto the bed.

She turned to him and shouted, "Now I see why you're this way. You've never been told no." Her hands on her hips, she stamped her foot. "Well, listen closely. I say NO!"

He was beside her in an instant. "Really, is that it? Is that what this is?" He grabbed her to him, his lips hard and demanding a response from her.

She pressed her lips together. Her fists rose on his chest to push him away. He ignored her and ran his tongue along the seam of her tightly compressed lips. One arm snaked around her waist, holding her to his body, bending her back-ward into him. His other hand moved down her back to the hem of her dress, touching the back of her knee, stroking up the bare flesh of her leg, lifting the fabric. Caressing her satin-covered buttock, he slid his hand along the firm globe. Her mouth opened to yell, and he thrust his tongue into her mouth. He crushed her to him. His hand moved ever so slowly from her bottom, around her hip, and into the front of her panties. He covered her mound, pressing against her, touching her center. He rubbed the tight curls. One finger ran along her seam, searching out her clitoris. His finger moved, awakening her. Rubbing and pressing, he knew where to touch her, ignite the flames of her desire.

Her fists stopped pushing at his chest. A heartbeat later, he felt her desire. Her hands opened on his chest, and she touched the tip of her tongue to his. He slipped two fingers into her core. Her palms slid up over his broad shoulders to the nape of his neck. Sarina's fingers entwined in his hair. Pulling him closer, she rose on her toes, pressing her hips forward. She moaned his name.

It took all his willpower to release her lips and take his fingers from her slick core as he moved away. Her brows furrowed as she looked at him, not understanding.

His voice was deep, sounding gruff to his ears. He wasn't unaffected. "I can have you whenever I want. You may stay in this room if that's your wish. Get dressed. We're going out this evening. Wear the emeralds."

She looked at him as if he'd gone mad. Shaken by her response to what he had done, her voice trembled, "Wh... What? Those—"

"Yes," he thundered, "they belong to me. To do with as I please, and it pleases me to see them on you."

She stamped her foot. "Ahhh." Oh, she was furious again. She couldn't even answer him.

He glanced down at his wristwatch. "You'd better hurry. You have three hours. Wear the pink gown. I'll have it brought to you." He turned and walked out the door.

She huffed and sat on the bed. "No. I won't," she shouted to his back, sounding just like one of her young students. Jason never turned. He closed the door behind him.

*I am not dressing. Oh, he is such a bully. Just because everyone else does what he says doesn't mean I have to. Let him come and drag me out.* She stopped and thought for a moment. What would he do if she didn't get dressed? In the end, she decided it was better to do as he wished.

This bedroom, though large, was much smaller than his master suite, but compared to her apartment, it was huge, with a separate tub and shower and a smaller dressing room. She hurried into the bathing chamber and turned on the shower. She pinned her hair loosely on top of her head and, afterward, wrapped a bath towel around herself.

Sarina found the beautiful pink gown with its chiffon overlay on the bed. The small number of clothes she had taken from Jason's room hung neatly in this dressing room. The low-cut gown had thin straps of silver and crystal beading at her shoulders, and the waist of the gown pulled tight with the same band of beading, making her look as if she were floating on air. The shoes were open-toe high heels, and across the front were crystal beads that matched the dress.

The emeralds had been left for her on the vanity. Sarina hadn't seen them since she sold them. Memories flooded her...

With a light knock on her bedroom door, Jason walked in. Sarina rose from the divan as he entered. He stopped, and his eyes traveled the length of her. "You are beautiful, a vision of loveliness. The goddesses would be jealous of you."

He stood so tall and magnificent in his black tuxedo,

white shirt, black bowtie, and his black hair and blue eyes. He was truly handsome, and that word wasn't enough to describe him. Adonis. Yes, Adonis.

He held out a pink wrap for her to take. "It isn't chilly now, but perhaps later, you may need this."

Jason led her downstairs and out the front door. She expected to get into the red Ferrari. Instead, a deep-burgundy Rolls Royce waited on the circular drive. On the front fenders were the flags of the king of San Destino. Both rear doors were open, and a guard stood at each. She stopped and looked up at Jason. His face was stern. In a husky, low voice, he said, "Come, don't make a scene."

She lifted her nose in the air. "I wasn't going to." A guard held the door, and she slid in. Jason walked around to the other side. Another guard at that door bowed his head to Jason. The privacy glass was clear, and Sarina could see a member of his personal guard in the front passenger seat.

She turned her head to him, a frown on her face. "Where are you taking me?"

He looked at her. "Have you forgotten?" The glimmer in his eyes couldn't be missed. "We're going to dinner."

She smiled at him as he took her hand, lacing her fingers with his as they rode in silence. The driver drove toward the airport, but not the main terminal. Again, she looked at Jason, a frown creasing her brow.

"All in good time, *cara mia.*"

On the tarmac, his private jet waited. The royal seal beamed in the sunlight. The limousine came to a stop. A red carpet laid on the ground, running from the limousine to the steps of the jet. Again, two guards came forward and opened both their doors. Jason exited and came around, taking her hand as they climbed the steps to board the plane. The interior décor of the plane mirrored the colors of the San Destino flag. He led her to an oversize leather seat. "I'll be right back. I want to talk with the pilot." He brushed a kiss on her temple.

While she sat, wondering where they were going, four men from his personal guard boarded the jet. They walked to the rear of the cabin and disappeared through a door.

"We'll take off shortly," Jason said as he took the seat opposite her.

"Why all the security?"

"No worries, *tesoro*, always when I travel. You won't know they're with us."

"Where are we going?" she asked, unable to keep the excitement from her voice. The jet's engines hummed to life. A soft vibration filled the cabin as the plane sped down the runway, taking off. Once the jet leveled, Sarina looked out the window. It was still light out, and they were over water. The cabin steward brought her white wine, and Jason chose the same. There was a silver tray with cheese, crackers, and grapes. Sarina nibbled on some cheese.

They were in the air a little over an hour when the captain spoke over the intercom. "We're cleared to land, so I'm beginning our descent, Your Majesty."

Sarina, too excited to contain herself, looked out the window. It wasn't quite dusk. She gasped, leaning closer to the oval window of the jet. She could make out the lagoon, and St. Mark's Square, famous throughout the world. "Oh! Venice! I can't believe it, Venice!" Joy bubbled in her voice.

He had flown her to one of the most romantic cities in the world. She couldn't contain her excitement. Once off the plane, they traveled by private boat to the Ducal Palace. Jason explained not only was it a hotel, but a museum and private residence as well. The entrance was on the Grand Canal. Sarina watched as gondolas glided by, the gondoliers singing to their passengers. Lights from the hotels and residences along the canal created a shimmering mirror effect on the water. The beautiful Venetian buildings, many with Juliet balconies, lined their facia.

Venice was magical, and Sarina felt as if she were transported to another time. She linked her arm through Jason's as they walked into the palace. The magic of Venice lay before her. He led her to a private dining room. Violin music filled the air with a lilting melody. Muted candlelight illuminated the room, flickering off the stone walls. Candelabras were lit at each of the tables, but only one table had been set for dinner. That one was on the balcony.

White lace and damask covered the round table. The cream-and-gold-bordered china plates sat on the table along with cut-crystal fluted glasses. An etched crystal bowl filled with clear water and fragrant flowers sat between long, tapered candles. Jason held out a gold-and-tapestry chair for Sarina. Once she sat, he chose the chair opposite her. That was the signal for the waiters to serve them.

She looked out over the Grand Canal. St. Mark's Square in the distance was lit, and the Basilica's dome reflected against the evening sky. Night had fallen. The lights of the hotels shone a muted yellow glow on the water. Sarina was thrilled to be here with Jason. He took her hand and kissed the tips of her fingers.

Her love for him was painful, squeezing her chest. Bittersweet. Now, with a sadness that would stay with her forever, she understood that expression. Her eyes stung with unshed tears. Unrequited love was painful and miserable. She knew that this was only a summer affair. After all, he was a king... and she was just a kindergarten teacher. She must keep that uppermost... *No! I won't think of that now. Nothing will spoil this time for me.*

AFTER DINNER, Jason took her to the famous Teatro La Fenice opera house to see La Traviata. She had never been to an opera, and though it was all in Italian, the music was so powerful and moving. After the performance, they strolled hand in hand through St. Mark's Square. Their private boat was waiting for them.

Jason turned to Sarina. "Would you like to ride in a gondola?"

The smile she gave him was brilliant, and she was almost jumping in her enthusiasm. "Yes! Yes! Can we?"

"We'll be tourists and ride under the Rialto Bridge." He smiled down at her.

"The magic of this night will always stay with me, Jason."

They went back to Marco Polo Airport and his jet on a private water boat.

Sarina, so tired from the day, fell asleep on the plane. Jason sat across from her, watching her curled up in a ball as she slept. He covered her with a blanket, tucking in the ends. *She's so headstrong in her own way. Under that angel's face and siren's body is a strong determination and, at the same time, an innocent gentleness.*

That she'd walked off the *Carmella* without any money showed him her courage and her strong family values. Had he not found her... what would have become of her? He didn't want to think of that. He was determined to keep her with him. Jason looked out the window, nodding his head, as a smile lifted the corner of his mouth. Funny, the opera tonight translated to *The Woman Who Stayed.*

The captain's voice over the intercom brought him back to the present. "Your Majesty, we're making our descent to San Destino."

Jason leaned over Sarina and gently woke her. She turned, opening her eyes, blinking, then giving him a smile. She kissed him on his cheek.

"Thank you for a wonderful night," she breathed.

He wouldn't take advantage of her. At the beach house, Jason walked her to the bedroom she chose. Taking her into his arms, he brushed a gentle kiss on her soft, sensuous lips. "*Buona notte, bella.* Good night, beautiful."

# CHAPTER 9

The following morning, Sarina awoke to find Jason reclining on the chaise lounge in her bedroom. "Come on, sleepyhead, wake up. I have a surprise for you. Get dressed. We can go riding."

"Riding?" She sat up in the bed, stretched, and pushed her hair out of her eyes. He pointed to a riding outfit that laid across the accent chair beside her bed.

"This morning, two of my horses were brought here from the palace stables. You said you like to ride."

"I do, but not… in… well, it's so expensive, so I haven't ridden." She shrugged a shoulder. "Not in a long time."

He rose from the chaise and came to the bed. Jason was already dressed for riding in a navy-blue polo shirt, his forearms bare except for a gold wristwatch, tan pants that hugged his body, knee-high brown leather riding boots, and a matching belt.

He stroked her cheek with his knuckle. She lifted her gaze to his and caught the way his blue eyes twinkled at her. Her face flamed when she realized how she'd stared at him. Jason brushed a kiss on her lips.

Her voice low, she couldn't look at him. "Yes, give me time to shower and dress."

He walked back to the chaise lounge and sat, crossing his long, muscular legs at the ankles. He clasped his hands behind his head. She looked at him questioningly.

"Well, I said you could sleep here, but I said nothing about not watching you."

She spun, and the satin and lace nightgown swirled around her. She walked into the bathing chamber, his laughter following her.

"Oh, you're impossible," she said as she went to turn on the shower, a smile on her lips and thoughts of Jason making her day bright.

A WEEK LATER, Sarina came downstairs to breakfast. Jason had made a pot of coffee, and there were delicious pastries on a silver tray. She chose a croissant and went out onto the patio, where they usually shared their morning meal. "Well, good morning, my sweet. I hope you slept well."

"Yes, thank you." She felt shy and unsure of herself. He touched her and held her, kissed her lightly, but never anything more than that, not since she said she wouldn't sleep with him.

"Today, I thought we would have a leisurely day, maybe take the boat out."

"Jason—"

He held a hand up. "Yes, I know we need to talk." Sitting on the patio in a white wrought-iron chair under a peach and cream umbrella, Jason gazed out at the sea below them.

"Sarina, stay with me. Stay for the rest of the summer."

How easy it would be to say yes and give in to the undeniable passion he brought out in her. In her heart, she knew there would never be anyone like him. *He's accustomed to taking what he wants. The women he knows... say yes and are... in a different class than me. Those women expect the finer things in life... giving them expensive gifts is part of it. He doesn't realize that isn't—nor will it ever be what I want. I want him to love me and find a way for us to be together.* Her breath caught, and her heart snagged as that thought burst into her consciousness.

"I'll fly you home and give you the money you need to send your sister to medical school. Let me do this for you. I want to make your life easier. I have the means. Allow me to help you."

Her head was spinning. "Jason, we've been over and over this. Maybe in your world, you can just throw money at someone to get what you want, but not me. You feel it's appropriate for me to take money from you. I can't accept that. I have a job, and I insist on paying you back for the airfare. And I'll pay for the clothes I've had to wear." She shrugged and briefly smiled before continuing, "You may have to wait a while for that, but I'll pay you back. I want—"

She stopped herself from blurting out that she loved him. Instead, she said, "I want to always remember you and this special time we shared. Taking money from you will turn it into… just sex… you know, your favorite phrase."

JASON CAME FORWARD out of his chair, and, crouching on his haunches, he held her hand. She sighed as the white fabric of his shorts stretched, the muscles in his bare, muscular thighs bunching, his shirt, open at the collar, exposing some of that delicious skin and molding to his pecs and abs.

He was so handsome and sexy. She breathed in his spicy, virile scent, unable to turn away from him. Her throat felt dry. What was he saying? She was so busy looking at him that she missed what he'd said.

"I'm sorry for those words… It's the way I am… I won't offer you any money or gifts. It's too late for you to find summer employment… Let's enjoy this time we have. Later today, we can go for a drive in the foothills. There's a nice restaurant where we can have a late lunch and walk around the vineyards. In the fall, they make the wine that's exclusively served at the palace."

*I have no willpower when it comes to him.* "At some point, I'll have to call my mother and let her know I'm all right."

He stood and went back to his seat, taking a sip of his coffee before he said, "Yes, of course, call your family. Let them know you're safe."

She'd have to do that, but not right now. Once they finished eating, they walked to his car and spent the entire day out.

In the evening, they drove back to the beach house. He led her upstairs and out to the patio off the master bedroom. A table draped with a damask cloth reaching to the stone floor had been set with china, silverware, and crystal flutes. The candles were lit, and their flames danced in the air. Next to one of the upholstered dining chairs stood a stand with a bottle of champagne cradled in the silver bucket.

Sarina walked over to the sideboard. It was covered with platters of lobster, crab, steamed vegetables, and salad. She turned to him, a puzzled look on her face.

He stood by her chair. Sliding it away from the table, he said, "Well, I called… to have this small supper prepated and waiting for us. There are some advantages to my being the king."

She smiled at that. "Yes, I guess so."

After dessert, he poured them each a brandy. He held out his hand, which she took, and they walked to the stone wall at the edge of the patio overlooking the Mediterranean and the secluded beach below. He placed the two brandy snifters on the ledge.

His arms circled her as she turned to look up into his handsome face. Her voice was soft. "I'll accept the airfare home, but only if you'll let me pay you back. I'll stay if you agree to those terms."

She was a pushover. Sarina knew it, he must know it too, but she couldn't help herself. She wanted as much time with him as she could get. Understanding came to her... how a person could turn their back on all they believed in and cling to another. She accepted the fact that, for him, it was just sex. After all, he kept reminding her of that. For her, it was love. She would take as many memories as she could with her. They would have to last her whole life.

"Please, Jason, love me, love me." Her voice husky and full of emotion, she wouldn't let him see her tears.

He held her close. "I'll make love to you all night long and every night, *cara mia.*"

He didn't understand, but she was greedy. She would desire him into eternity and would take this time, keeping it in her heart forever. Jason scooped her up into his muscular arms, carrying her to his bed. Seven nights without him, she was crazy with need for him.

"Sorry I ripped your dress in my lust."

She gazed up into his blue eyes. "That's okay. Rip the rest."

His smile broadened, and the fabric tore down her back. Her open palms slid up his shirt. Reaching for the top button, he brushed them away, moving faster.

Her fingers trembled as they grasped his belt buckle. Then, she rubbed her hand over the bulge of his erection. "Very nice." She unzipped his pants while he reached to brush the tatters of her dress down her body to pool at her feet. She knew they wouldn't make it to the bed.

"I don't know if I can go slow with you, Sarina." He held her waist, and she lifted her leg. He pulled her to him so that she wrapped her legs around his narrow waist. Once Sarina decided to stay, she embraced the feelings Jason brought out in her.

The next day, Jason would be gone for several hours. He'd planned "a day at the spa" to be delivered to her. A half-dozen women walked into the master bath carrying all sorts of goodies for her. A spa day was something she heard about but never had the pleasure to indulge in… and it was a pleasure. She was handed a flute of flavored mineral water. The tub was filled, and the jets turned on. She relaxed in the swirling water. Then she was given the most soothing massage with warm stones. Her toenails and fingernails were painted, she was waxed and pampered, and her hair was trimmed and styled. She indulged in this decadent experience, wanting to please Jason.

Jason was at his office in the palace. He was in a rush to get back to Sarina. Her spa day was just about over, and he intended to surprise her with dinner and the symphony. He was almost done when Prince Henri, Catarina's husband, was announced. The three of them had a close relationship. Henri wasn't only a relative, but one of Jason's closest advisors. He knew what Henri wanted to discuss. He also knew that Cat had put him up to it. Jason wouldn't make it easy for him.

Sarina was his business. Jason was always discreet and kept his lovers away from his duties. He couldn't help keeping Sarina at the beach house or if he desired here at the palace—that was his privilege. He felt comfortable with Sarina and wanted her in his life.

His eyebrows rose, bringing him up short. It was completely unexpected. He wanted her in his life? How so? Just until he was over her… right? No. He knew that there was no getting over Sarina. *She's in my blood. When did that happen?* He'd been fooling himself. It happened from the beginning. When she sold the jewels, yes, he was furious over that, but now he understood the anger was directed at her because she wanted to leave him. It had nothing to do with the jewelry. It was because she was walking out on him. Well, that would never happen again. *I made sure of that. She now has her own personal guards. They're discreet; she doesn't suspect.*

At the palace, when he'd taken her to his apartment and bed—with her first touch—all his anger had evaporated. It was replaced by a steamy, fiery passion that he had never known with any other woman. She invaded his dreams. His waking hours were filled with her.

He'd been tortured those nights when she was determined to sleep apart from him. Denying him her luscious body, he had missed her next to him, reaching out and feeling the empty space in the bed. He'd walked around in a semi-aroused state for days. Even now, all he wanted was to be buried deep inside her heat, searching out her pleasure points, feeling her contracting around him, loving him. *Yes! I want her to love me.*

The man who sat across from him cleared his throat. "Henri, all in good time. You go take care of Catarina."

Henri looked at Jason questioningly. "Is she so different?"

He gave his brother-in-law the *I'm king* look, then sighed. "Tonight, I'm taking Sarina to the symphony. Why don't you and Cat join us? Yes, do that. You both can meet her." He rose, grabbed his suit jacket, and left Henri in his office.

Sarina, a book in her hands, was lounging on the terrace

when Jason walked in, his jacket slung over his shoulder. He leaned against the doorframe with one leg crossed in front of the other. He drank in her beauty, unable to hide the tenderness in his eyes. Sarina looked up and gasped, her smile alive with delight. She jumped up and ran into his arms.

"Oh, Jason, it was wonderful. Thank you for today." She reached on tiptoes and brushed her lips against his cheek. He bent and moved his mouth over hers in a slow, tender kiss.

She sighed, parting her lips as her lethal body leaned into him. His custom-made jacket fell to the floor. He lifted her into his arms, kissing the satin column of her neck. Carrying her inside, his lips descended to meet her sensuous mouth, devouring her as he walked to his bed. He gently stood her on her feet as his fingers unfastened her silk blouse, button by button, revealing more of the satin skin.

She shivered, and he knew it wasn't from being cold. His kisses moved to the column of her beautiful neck. It felt like heaven to him. Her blouse was open, and when he heard her breath catch in her throat, he knew it was because of what his fingers were doing to her sensitive breasts. The need to replace his fingers with his mouth drove him. He stopped long enough to take her blouse from her, sliding the satin straps of her bra down her arms. The tips of her breasts were hard pebbles pointed against the lacy fabric. He unclasped the bra and sent it sailing across the room.

She laughed, a throaty laugh that shot desire, sharp and hot, into his groin, making him instantly hard. He went back to what had become his favorite pastime, making Sarina quiver with need for him and listening to the music of her moans.

He circled one nipple, sucking it into his mouth, then brought more of her areola into his mouth, licking the swollen bud. He gently eased her down onto the mattress. The soft sound of her moan inflamed him. He was so hard;

he wasn't sure he could continue this without sinking into her heat.

Red, silky hair streamed across the pillow, her head rolling from side to side. He bent to her other breast, licking and nibbling on the nipple. He slid her skirt down her shapely legs and removed her panties. His lips kissed a path down her belly to the curve of her hip.

Sarina held him closer, pushing his shirt off. She half-sat and unzipped his trousers. He took over, and in one motion, his pants and boxers were down his legs and thrown to the floor. Sarina ran the pad of one nail-polished finger along his rigid length, looking into his eyes. Her emerald-green gaze burned with desire, almost taking his breath away. Her boldness was his undoing.

He had to be in her. All of him now! He reached for the condom on the bedside table, ripped the foil packet open, and rolled on the protection. He knelt over her, spreading her legs with one knee as he kissed her beautiful mouth. Caressing her belly, he moved his hand lower until one finger found her center.

She was hot and wet, ready for him. He couldn't wait another second. He had to be in that tight heat. She sighed at his deep, sure thrust, meeting each of his penetrating thrusts. Her hips rose, and her arms looped around his neck. She lifted her legs to lock her ankles around his waist, wanting all of him. "Yes, more. Faster."

He slowed.

She moaned.

He stopped.

She groaned, "Jason, no."

He wasn't sure he could control himself buried deep in her.

She arched her back. Her warm breath was at his ear. "Please, I need you." She rolled her hips.

He smiled, then said, "You have no patience."

"Oh, you." She moved her hips, beckoning once more.

That was Jason's undoing. He thrust a half-dozen more times before she screamed in her pleasure. Jason waited. When her shudders slowed, he looked into her passion-glazed eyes.

"Again?" he said and thrust into her, slowly at first.

Sarina wanted none of that. She was wild.

Jason pulled out, only leaving the tip in. She moaned, her hands reaching his buttocks, pulling him. He plunged into her heat. Faster and faster, this time he wouldn't hold back, and he took them both soaring over the edge. Sarina was asleep almost before her last shudder of pleasure.

Jason rolled to his side and pulled that lethal body closer into his arms. He smoothed the silky mass of red curls from her brow, her dark lashes fanning her cheeks. *This is where you belong in my bed, in my arms always.* He fell asleep.

SARINA AWOKE in Jason's embrace, her back against his massive chest, wishing that it could always be like this. He'd taught her about passion and lust. She had no idea that she was so brazen. There was nothing she didn't want to try with Jason. She knew she loved him, even now being satisfied. If he touched her, she would make love with him again.

She turned slightly when she felt him hard against her buttocks.

He leaned over her shoulder and smiled. "I can't get enough of you, *tesoro mio*, my treasure." He kissed her. Jason's hand skimmed over her. His long fingers were at the juncture of her legs. Brushing and stroking, one of his fingers moved in. She needed nothing more. Sarina was ready for him.

He teased her, kissing the side of her neck as he moved his finger further into her, making her sigh. She held his forearm, opening herself for more of the pleasure he gave.

Kissing her neck, he gently nudged her onto her back. He rolled on top of her. She reached up, pulling his head down for a kiss, and slipped her tongue into his mouth. He moved onto his back, taking her with him. She stopped, not sure what he wanted.

He said, "You lead."

She was confused, but the smile he gave her sent her pulse racing.

"Like this, my sweet." He guided her leg so that she straddled him. He held her waist, lifting her to gently lower her an inch at a time onto his rigid body. Her eyes opened wide in surprise. His hands glided to her hips, fingers splayed, pulling her. His words encouraging her. "Just... yes... ahh... like that."

She slid slowly down his shaft, hesitant at first, then she caught the rhythm, feeling all new sensations. Sarina set the pace as the coil in her belly tightened, erupting into waves and waves of bliss as a powerful climax only Jason could give her started deep in her center.

Her head fell back, her long hair streaming down her back as she swayed and bounced on him.

He held her breasts, exciting her nipples. "Your breasts are beautiful, so big." He trailed one finger down her torso, further over her abdomen, to where his dark black hair mingled with her newly trimmed tuft of red hair. He slid his finger into her, pressing on her clit.

"Oh, Jason." She loved this, what he did to her. The waves of her climax came from deep within, surprising her with their intensity.

"I feel you coming. You're so tight and hot." He held her

hips to his and shouted out his own release. She fell forward, and his arms came around her, holding tight.

"We won't make it to the symphony." He brushed a kiss on her brow. "I'll call Henri. He and Cat were going to meet us." Again, they slept.

Sometime after midnight, they woke up starving. Sarina went with him to the kitchen, where they made an omelet. She sliced a crusty loaf of bread, cubed some cheese, peeled an orange, and placed it on a plate. They sat in the kitchen and ate out of the same plate and drank wine out of the same glass. "Has your sister ever met... your... the... other women..." Sarina's voice trailed off, and she lowered her eyes.

"You want to know about my other women?"

She glanced up at him. "No. Yes. Yes, you said you never brought them to San Destino."

"No, I never cared enough to bring anyone here."

"Well, I guess it's a moot point. You found me here."

His grin expanded into a dazzling smile before he said, "The best thing that's ever happened to me was finding you on the road to the palace." They laughed and talked while eating, then they went back to bed. Some time passed before they fell asleep.

DURING THE LAZY days of summer, Jason and Sarina fell into a routine, as lovers often did. Some days he would take her on long drives, showing her San Destino as only he could. She hadn't realized how large the island was, with two international airports and three smaller domestic ones. The royal family owned a beautiful palace in the mountains on the east side of the island. They packed their own suitcase and prepared to spend a few days there. Jason wanted to show her all the wonders of San Destino. Jason was proud of all that he'd accomplished in the thirteen years since he ascended the throne.

Wherever they stopped, the people would come out to greet him. She saw how much they loved their king. He listened to them and took care of any matters that concerned them. Women would bring out their babies, and he happily held them, posed for selfies with them. She saw how good he was with children. Jason was relaxed and happy when he was out and about the island.

The people would give him fruits and vegetables from their gardens. He was gracious in accepting them. The food never went to waste. He and Sarina would use what they could, and the rest would go to the palace. There was no need for food banks, as he'd explained to Sarina. San Destino was prosperous. That had been his utmost priority. There was no hunger or homelessness in his country.

On one particular outing, Jason wanted to spend the night at his lodge. The rustic hunting lodge lay beside a lake. Again, she was taken aback—the lodge was a two-story, massive, sixteen-bedroom home sprawled out on the shore of a vast freshwater lake. Sarina couldn't even see the other side of the lake. They arrived in the early evening; the lodge was rustic but with all the comforts of home. The caretakers had the lights on, and the bed in the master bedroom turned down. There was even a meal prepared should they be hungry. "They really take care of you, don't they?"

He pulled her into his arms and kissed her. "I like the way you take care of me."

She leaned into his muscular body and felt him hard against her belly. At the feel of his desire, her own grew as heat spread, preparing her for him. She didn't care that they were in the kitchen. Her hands went to the buttons of his shirt.

He pulled her up hard against his body, laced his fingers under her buttocks. "*Cara mia*, wrap your legs around me."

Her center throbbed as a long, low moan escaped her parted lips. She pulled the tails of his unbuttoned shirt out of his slacks. As he walked her over to the kitchen table, his foot shoved the chair out of the way, and he sat her on the table's edge. Sarina unbuttoned his waistband. A slow smile spread across her lips as her palm ran over the bulge of his erection.

Jason brushed her hands away and pulled her blouse over her head. Her nipples strained against the sheer black bra. He kissed her collarbone and unclasped her bra, freeing her breasts. He circled the crest of one, sucking the nipple into his mouth, flicking it with his tongue.

A moan escaped her.

Jason treated the other breast to the same delight. She slid his zipper down and caressed his magnificent erection.

He swatted her hands away. "No, no, my sweet, there is something I've wanted to do all day."

"What could that be?" She held his shoulders.

He unzipped her skirt, and with his arm around her waist, he lifted her enough to slide the fabric down her legs. The garment fell silently to the floor. He left her sheer black thong on along with her peep-toe high heels.

"Lie down for me, my sweet." He hovered over her.

She breathed in his scent, and her hands cupped the back of his head, fingers digging into the thick black hair. His mouth covered hers. Their tongues tangled, and he lay her on the table, his hand on her breast, his fingers teasing her nipple as he stood between her spread knees.

Sarina panted, and on a half moan, Jason took the nipple into his mouth, teasing the peak with the tip of his tongue. She arched her back, holding him to her breast.

She bit her bottom lip, looking at him. He raised one black eyebrow as she felt his hands on her ankles. Breathing became difficult as she gazed into his handsome face, anticipating what he would do next. She almost climaxed. He kissed her belly, his hands moving up her legs and positioning her closer to the edge of the table. A devilish smile reached into his blue eyes as he knelt and nudged her legs farther apart, his hot mouth on the inside of her knee, kissing higher and higher, his tongue leaving a trail of heat as he reached her inner thigh. She groaned when he stopped.

"I thought of nothing but this all day. I crave your taste on my tongue."

She was on fire. Her breasts ached, the nipples stiff points. She moaned, not holding anything back. "Yes, I need you."

Then his hot breath was at the apex of her legs. She moaned again. Jason rubbed his thumb over the fabric of her thong before he hooked his fingers in the elastic and slid her thong down and off her legs, removing her shoes as he went.

She was so primed for him, her red curls glistened with her desire. He licked her… Sarina's sexual tension was palpable. Sex had never been as amazing as it was every time with his red-haired beauty. She writhed on the table, and her siren's call grew louder.

He was bursting to be inside her heat. Jason pushed himself to greater control, taking Sarina's knees and gently nudging them further apart. He lifted her legs to rest on his shoulders. Her moans drove him higher and higher as he slid both hands under her buttocks, bringing her closer to his mouth. Jason parted her with his thumbs, stroking his tongue over her clit, circling that bud once, twice before sliding his tongue into her heat, tasting the honey that waited for him. He felt the very first contraction on his tongue; he thrust further into her heat.

Sarina raised her knees, the heels of her feet pressing against his back. Holding her to his mouth, licking and sucking, he heard her moans growing longer and louder, feeling her body tense as the waves of her contractions came faster. She screamed in pleasure. Her fingers played in his hair as her legs relaxed on his shoulders.

"Want to come again?" He slid two fingers into her vagina, finding that one spot in her honeyed heat to give her the greatest orgasm.

She whimpered, "Oh God, Jason, yes."

He crooked his finger, pressing and rubbing at the same time his tongue flicked her clit. She held his head. Her fingers pressed him closer. He sucked her clit and rubbed her g-spot. She lifted her hips. He held her down and sucked again.

"Jason, oh Jason, too much, I ca—" She screamed as her climax took over, going on and on, stroking his fingers in her heat. Gradually, the shudders slowed as he sucked her clit, sliding his fingers deeper into her wet heat, giving his beautiful siren another wave of spasms.

"Jason..." she whispered his name on a sigh.

He kissed her abdomen and stood, retrieving the foil packet from his pants pocket, never taking his eyes off Sarina. Her body flushed with pleasure. He toed off his shoes and in one motion, dropped his slacks and underwear. Naked, he lifted her in his arms. "We can't make it to the bed," he said and carried her draped around him to the nearest wall. Hearing her sigh his name made him harder and hotter than he had ever been. He couldn't remember a time when his need was so great, unable to wait any longer, needing to be in her searing heat. His arm came out from under Sarina's legs.

Her toes touched the kitchen floor, her silky arms rising around his neck. He kissed her mouth, and his tongue coaxed hers to play. Jason lifted her and instinctively, her curvy legs slid around his hips as the tip of his erection rested at the entrance of her core. He thrust.

A moan on her lips, her head fell back. Her lethal body wrapped around him. He kissed her taut nipples, pressing the curve of her back against the wall. Jason levered himself to go deeper, inch by inch, thrust by thrust, embedding himself into Sarina's blazing heat.

Her eyes opened. The emerald green held bliss in their depths and a promise of ecstasy for him. His frenzied strokes had Sarina crying out her pleasure. The waves of her climax clenched around him, taking all he had into her. She turned her head and kissed the crook of his neck.

Jason groaned and shuddered into Sarina, his laced fingers holding her buttocks. Gradually, her legs slipped from his hips, and her feet touched the floor. He leaned against her, his forehead touching hers, holding Sarina up until their breathing returned to normal. He looked into those emerald-green eyes, touched her flushed cheek, and brushed a gentle kiss on her lips. He took her hand, and naked, they walked up the stairs to his bedroom. He pulled the covers around them, and they slept.

In the morning, they had breakfast at the lodge before driving back to the beach house. Jason stopped his car in the plaza of a small town. The people were cheering and soon, there was a large crowd around him. Sarina always felt uncomfortable, but he would take her hand, and she would walk with him. Everyone was friendly, although she was sure they wondered who she was. No one ever asked or said anything. He would just introduce her as Sarina Moore.

On this bright sunny day, an elderly woman came up to Sarina and handed her a beautiful bouquet of roses. "From my garden for you."

"Oh. Thank you. They're lovely," Sarina said as she graciously accepted the bouquet.

The older woman told Sarina how she remembered the day that His Majesty King Filippo was born. Church bells rang out through all of San Destino, and people came out of their homes cheering. She hoped one day to see his wedding as well.

Sarina smiled at the woman and looked at Jason from the corner of her eye. He smiled when he took the older woman's gnarled hand, brought it to his lips, and kissed it. The old lady was so flustered, she curtsied to him while the townspeople cheered. Jason put his arm around Sarina's waist and walked her to the car. He waved to the people. They drove off in his red Ferrari.

# CHAPTER 10

The time was fast approaching for Sarina to return home, prepare her classroom, move on with her life. But for now—Sarina reclined on the cream-and-orange-striped cushion of a patio lounge chair. Her legs crossed at the ankle, as she picked up a glossy magazine from the side table.

Her eyes rounding, she jolted forward. On the cover, staring back at her—a photo of her and Jason. The tagline read something about the Playboy King and his new mistress. Snarling, she threw the magazine to the floor. She stood and took an abrupt step, stopped—she never bothered Jason with calls while he was at his office at the palace, but this was too much. A phone was always nearby. She pressed a single number on the receiver and called Jason.

"You miss me already? I won't be much longer."

A short time later, he came home and sauntered out onto the patio, a grin spread across his lips. She hurried to him, holding up the mangled magazine. "What if my mother or sister sees this? What if one of our neighbors sees it and tells her? I can't believe how stupid I've been not to realize these photos can make it to the US."

"Calm down, my sweet. You knew that sooner or later we would be photographed. Why haven't you called your mother? You've been talking about that. Explain where—"

She stood before him. Again, she threw the magazine to the floor as she said, "Oh, yes. Why don't I? Well… let's see, hmm… what will I say?"

Her breasts heaved, pulling the blue silk fabric of her blouse tight. She wore white slacks and high-heel stilettos. The top of her head only reached his chin as she paced in front of him. He was going to strip her right here on the patio, lay her on the warm tile floor…

She stared into his eyes, as her green ones filled with anger. Sarina placed one sleeveless arm across her waist, the elbow of her other arm resting in her cupped hand, her pointing finger tapping her flushed cheek. "Oh. I know." He heard the snark in her voice. "Hi, Mom, it's me, your level-headed daughter. I just wanted to let you know I'm fine. Do you remember that job where I was going to be a companion for a grandmother? Well, it wasn't what I thought it was. She wanted me to sleep with her grandson, so I ran away. And by the way, I met this king. I sold some jewelry he gave me. I was trying to buy a ticket to get home to you. He won't let me go, and now I'm living with him openly, and I may be pregnant, but don't worry, I'll be home next month. Bye, for now. Kisses."

He couldn't miss the fury in her voice by the end of that tirade. Her cheeks were flushed, and her eyes shot green fire at him.

His deep voice ominously quiet. "What do you mean you might be pregnant?"

She gazed up, eyes round. Sarina shouted, "That's all you heard?"

"That, *cara mia*, is the most important part. Well, are you? Are you?" he shouted back. *This beauty before me is the only person who can make me lose my temper.*

She dropped onto the chaise lounge, with her head bowed. "I'm not sure," she mumbled. "I haven't had my period since I arrived here… and now—well, I can't be sure of anything." She tilted her head back, looking up at him. "You always use a condom, and I was a virgin." She shrugged one blue, silk–covered shoulder. "That's why I never thought about birth control."

He nodded, then pursed his lips. "Ummah." An image of him taking her to his bed at the palace, when she was first brought back from the airport, flashed before his mind's eye. *Not once, but twice without protection.*

He knelt by her chair, caressed her cheek, then he took her hands from her lap. "Shush. First, let's see if you are expecting my baby… I'm sure my sister keeps a pregnancy test or two here. If not, we'll get one." He rose. "Let me look in her suite while you wait here."

He brushed a stray auburn curl away from her cheek.

He went to Catarina's suite. In the medicine cabinet, he found what he was looking for, and it hadn't expired. *Leave it to Cat to always be prepared.*

Walking back to the patio, he handed Sarina the package, his voice calm. "Here, it's in English. Read the directions and use this."

She stood, smoothed her slacks down, and walked to the bathroom.

Jason paced the floor of the spacious master bedroom, glancing at his wristwatch. *What's taking her so long?*

When Sarina walked into the room, he said, "Do not look so forlorn… I can see by your expression that you carry my child."

Raising her hand, she began, "Before you say anything else, I've decided to keep this baby. I'm going to raise it, with my mother's help. You don't have to worry about anything. No one need ever know."

His eyebrows shot up, with his voice deceivingly calm. "Really, little thief, so now you want to steal my heir?"

"What are you talking about?"

"We'll announce our engagement, and you'll marry me within the month."

She stood there, her eyes rapidly blinking. She lifted her chin, held his gaze with her own, and said, "Again… orders? You decided. You didn't even ask. Not even a, a… will you marry me? No. It's you will marry me. Autocratic as always!"

Jason looked at her so petite and worried, but then… she could turn into a tiger at a moment's notice and that acid tongue… He preferred when she used it to lick his body and excite him.

Sarina walked to the couch by the fireplace and dropped down onto the silk-covered cushion. He sat next to her, took her hand, his thumb rubbing along her delicate wrist. "You're right. It was insensitive of me." Jason went down on one knee. "Miss Moore, would you do me the honor of marrying me? Be my wife… my queen?"

He held his breath. *Would she refuse me?* When he said queen, her eyes got as big as two saucers.

"Jason, are you absolutely sure you want this?"

"Yes, more than anything, I want you to marry me. Share my life." The smile playing around his lips broadened before he said, "I promise you won't regret it."

He saw the fear in her eyes and then the gradual smile before she said, "Yes! Yes, I'll marry you."

Standing, he slid his hands around her tiny waist, lifting her to her feet, kissing her. "Good. Now, call your mother. I'll telephone my sister. Catarina will know best how to proceed with the announcement."

He was all business again, taking charge of the situation as he was bred to. "We'll have dinner with the family this evening. I want you to meet Cat and Henri... their three children."

Her hand lifted to her brow, fingers pressing on her forehead. *Is she going to faint?* This time, he'd be prepared to catch her.

She took a breath. "What time is it in Connecticut?"

He listened to the slow exhalation, realizing how nervous she was. He caressed her cheek, feeling the slight flush. "I know this will be most difficult for you..." He brushed his lips on her brow. "I'll leave you to your call—"

He stopped. "Perhaps your mother and sister will fly out... I'll send my jet for them. I know it'll come as a surprise to find out you're engaged." He chuckled in an attempt to relieve her nervousness. "Just say... you met... a man... Try to leave out the rest."

She nodded, a smile raising the corners of her mouth.

"I'll leave you to your call."

After talking with his sister, he decided that they would have dinner in Henri and Catarina's apartments at the palace so that the children wouldn't be disrupted from their bedtime schedule.

Catarina and Henri were charming and most gracious to Sarina. Once dinner was over, the children were sent to bed with their nannies. The four adults sat in the living room. All but Sarina had a brandy. She had sparkling water. Jason said that they'd decided to marry and wanted to have the ceremony at the Cathedral within the month. There was no mention of why the hurry. When Jason wanted something, he got what he wanted, and he wanted Sarina as his wife. The evening went well, and then, rather than drive down to the beach house, Jason and Sarina spent the night in his apartment at the palace. As they undressed for bed, Jason thought, *This is where we created the life she's carrying. Very appropriate that my heir was conceived in this bed.*

The next morning, an appointment was made for Sarina to see the royal family's doctor. Jason prepared the announcement that his personal secretary William would give to the press of the upcoming marriage of His Majesty King Filippo Alfonso Nicolas Giovanni Stefano of the House of Donato, to Miss Sarina Moore of Connecticut in the United States. The date and location would be forthcoming. The press release was finished.

Before breakfast, Jason's secretary arrived. He entered the study in Jason's private apartment, along with a footman. The footman held a silver tray and, on the tray, a small blue velvet box. "Sir, as you requested." His secretary gave a slight bow and handed Jason the box.

"Thank you, William. Here is the announcement. You may go now."

The two men left the room, and Jason opened the lid and smiled. He pocketed the jewelry box and went to meet Sarina for breakfast.

She was on the terrace, her red hair tied back from her face, wearing a creamy pale-yellow dress with shoulder ties and a ruffle at the hemline. She plated fresh-cut melon.

"Good morning, my sweet. You look too young to be the wild woman in my bed last night."

The plate rattled, and she bowed her head. Jason wrapped his arms around her waist and kissed the side of her neck. "How do you feel?"

"I feel great but starving. Would you like some fruit? Coffee?" she asked.

"Yes, coffee, please." The early morning sun turned her red locks to fire as she placed the plate on the table by her seat. She poured two cups of coffee and brought them to the table.

"Come here," he said as he pulled Sarina onto his lap, kissing her. "We'll take an official photo in two days' time. The press will be brought into the throne room for a photo opportunity... and to see your ring... You know you may choose whatever you wish as an engagement ring." He paused when her gaze met his. Her fingers played in the hair at the nape of his neck. "But perhaps..." He slipped the box out of his jacket pocket and opened the lid.

Sarina gasped. "Oh."

"My father gave this ring to my mother on the day I was born."

"Oh, my, it's beautiful."

"If you're agreeable, I would like this to be your engagement ring."

"Yes." She wiggled on his lap and hugged his neck.

He took her hand. "Allow me. I think it will fit." He slid the six-carat, heart-shaped diamond onto her finger. "Perfect," he said, kissing her lips. "You don't worry about the wedding preparations. The most you'll need to do is pick out your dress. I'll do the rest."

"Okay, Jason."

"I've contacted a local designer. They'll be here shortly. You'll need casual and formal wear for all occasions as well as shoes, purses, hats, lingerie—"

"I already have a room full of clothes."

Jason laughed at that and said, "You'll need more."

Sarina took a bite of melon.

"I know this may be overwhelming for you, but we'll get through it together. I've assigned some men from my personal guard to you."

~

IN THE AFTERNOON, Jason and Sarina drove to the cathedral and met with the cardinal. She felt quite nervous, but when Sarina saw the aisle she would have to walk up, she clutched Jason's arm. The cardinal was a cheerful man. "This cathedral was built in 1354, and since that time, every king and queen of San Destino has married here."

Jason had arranged for the royal jet to take Sarina to Milan so she could meet with the famous designer who would make her wedding dress. Catarina had offered to go with Sarina, but Sarina wanted to go alone. Catarina had too much to do, and Sarina didn't want to add to her schedule. Sarina's measurements were taken, and an appointment was made for her to return in two weeks for a fitting, then a final fitting one week later. The designer had sketched a fairytale dress for her and would personally deliver the dress to San Destino.

Catarina was busy making the arrangements for a grand ball that would be held the evening before the wedding. The wedding luncheon and the wedding ball. There was quite a bit of preparations that needed her expert attention. Invitations needed to be printed and delivered. Sleeping arrangements for the guests needed to be made.

Her soon-to-be sister-in-law spoke over the phone with the designer. She knew there was a lot of pressure on him to have the dress ready in three weeks as opposed to the normal four to six months that such a dress might normally take. Once Sarina said, "I do," not only would she be Jason's wife, but she would become the queen of San Destino. All the preparations were going well. Sarina realized Catarina was in her element, just like her brother, making decisions and giving orders.

A few days later, Sarina and Catarina stood on the

parquet wood floor in the pink-and-mint-green-colored ballroom. Trimmed with gold, it was the largest of the palace's ballrooms, a magnificent two-story room with gilded mirrors interspersed between floor-to-ceiling windows.

Sarina's gaze was drawn to the ceiling where a fresco was painted. No less than eight crystal chandeliers hung between the intricate gold detailing. The room was breathtaking. Against the walls were velvet-covered divans and silk-upholstered chairs.

"You're good for my brother. I know he would be the last to admit it but believe me when I say I've never seen him so happy."

Sarina glanced at Catarina. Jason and Sarina had decided to keep her pregnancy from their families. Only the royal gynecologist knew she was expecting the heir to the throne of San Destino.

"Thank you for that. I… I've been concerned… that I'm pressuring him into

something—"

There was never any doubt in Sarina's mind that she would marry him. She loved him and would always want to be with him.

Catarina shook her head of black hair. "Believe me, there isn't anyone who could pressure Filippo to do anything he doesn't choose to."

WHEN JASON MET Sarina's mother Elizabeth, he knew instantly what Sarina would look like when she was older. Mrs. Moore was as petite as his fiancée and as beautiful. The three Moore women all had red hair and various shades of green eyes. Elizabeth's eye color was more of a hazel, Julia's eyes were a unique shade of moss green; and Sarina's were that vibrant emerald green. Julia was taller than her mother and sister by about five inches. She was just as beautiful as her sister but got her height from their father.

Sarina took her mother and sister to visit with the designer that would make Julia's maid of honor dress and the mother of the bride dress. Jason had suggested that she take them to some of the local boutiques for clothes, shoes, handbags, and any other items they needed. He was careful how he phrased that suggestion. He knew how Sarina felt about money, but he had his own personal wealth and wanted his fiancée and her family to feel comfortable at the social events they would be attending.

A week before the wedding, there was so much going on. In a few days, their wedding celebrations would begin. Sarina and Jason planned a private informal dinner in his apartment for her mother, Julia, Catarina, and Henri.

Jason felt comfortable with Sarina's family and pleased that they were so supportive of each other. They were close, each doing their part to help one another. Jason and Sarina had picked a maid of honor gift to present to Julia this evening after dinner. They had also picked out a gift for her mother. Sarina was excited and couldn't wait for dinner to be over.

When Jason had first mentioned that he wanted to present each with a gift of jewelry, Sarina wasn't sure how she felt about it. "It's a tradition to give the members of the bridal party a gift of remembrance. Your mother is also in the bridal party, so I feel we should present her with a memento as well."

He convinced her it was the proper thing to do. His jeweler met them at the palace. For Julia, they chose a diamond-and-amethyst pair of earrings with a matching bracelet. For Catarina, they chose a ruby-and-diamond broach, and for her mother, they chose a pair of diamond earrings with two diamond extensions so they could be worn as studs or mid-length and brushing her shoulders for very formal evenings. For Henri, they chose a solid-gold wristwatch, engraved with the monarch's crown, an *F* and *S* intertwined, and the date of their wedding.

Then Jason and Sarina chose gifts for the children and his cousin, who was also walking with the bridal party.

That night before bed, Sarina walked into the large dressing room. Jason was unbuttoning his shirt when she turned her back to him and moved her hair out of the way. "Can you please unzip me?"

He dropped a kiss on the back of her neck. "Yes, my sweet."

"I'm sorry I don't have a gift for you," she said in a low voice.

He kissed down her neck as the zipper revealed her velvet-soft skin to him, dropping kisses down her spine. "Your present to me is the baby you carry." He pulled her against his bare chest, hugging her to him, skimming the rim of her ear with the tip of his tongue, kissing her jaw, the side of her neck. He ran his tongue over her shoulder and pushed her dress off, turning her in his arms; the dress fell to the floor. She heated his blood as no other ever had, and to see her in the frilly bra and panties, the scent of her filled his head—he fell to a knee, his arms going around her tiny waist, dragging her to him, and he kissed her belly.

The following day was a mad rush of activities to prepare for the pre-wedding ball, which was that night. Formal gowns and tiaras had been chosen. The day and evening passed in a blur of activities.

∼

THE DAY of the wedding dawned bright and beautiful. The air was clean and cool for August. Jason's apartment comprised of well over thirty rooms, including eight bedroom suites. Sarina had spent the night with her mother and sister in their suite at the palace.

Julia dressed in a yellow mermaid-style gown that hugged her curves and flared at the bottom into a small train. Her auburn hair pulled away from her face, ringlets cascading down her back, the only embellishment yellow and purple flowers in her hair. She wore the amethyst and diamond earrings and matching bracelet Jason and Sarina had given her.

Mrs. Moore looked beautiful in a turquoise watered-silk gown with a beaded bodice. Her red hair was swept into a bun. Sarina never saw her mother look more beautiful.

Jason's secretary arrived with a large wooden, hinged box. "His Majesty has asked me to deliver these to you, ma'am." He bowed and left the room. Sarina's fingers trembled as she opened the envelope and read the note.

In his bold handwriting, she read, *Wear these for me. Forever Yours, Jason.*

She opened the box and gasped. Necklace, earrings, and bracelet gleamed, sparkled, and winked at her. Diamonds! The design was identical to the tiara she would wear. Her engagement ring, for today, was on her right hand. Jason had hired the jeweler Sarina had sold the emeralds to to design her wedding band. Jason wanted the ring to be a surprise. Each time she looked down at her hand, she was amazed, feeling as if she were dreaming and would wake up, sad that it was only a dream.

"Mom, pinch me. I want to be sure this is real."

Her mother laughed. "It's real, dear, but could you pinch me to be sure?"

Julia chuckled. "You're both going to be black and blue if

you aren't careful with all that pinching." They laughed and hugged each other.

Catarina came in to check on their progress. She wore a pink gown with a small train, her ruby-and-diamond tiara, ruby-and-diamond earrings, and around her neck a matching necklace. A sash with the colors of the Royal Family of San Destino lay from her left shoulder to her right hip. The broach she and Jason gave Catarina was pinned at her shoulder, holding the sash in place. She was beautiful with her black-as-night hair swept into an intricate chignon.

It was time. Sarina put on her wedding dress, a flowing ball gown with a sweetheart neckline. The bodice was covered in crystals and pearls; from the waist on down, the design of the crystal and pearls continued around the gown, along the hem, and on the fifteen-foot train. The date of their wedding was embroidered on a satin band.

The veil had its own unique history, having been in Jason's family for hundreds of years. Catarina had given it to her, explaining how each bride of the House of Donato had worn the veil since their great-great-great-grandmother had it made for her wedding. The veil extended six feet past the train, the edge a band of re-embroidered lace with crystals and pearls interspersed.

Sarina's mother had brought some of the lace from her wedding gown for Sarina to incorporate into her gown. "Your father and I were happy and just as in love as the day we met. Wear some of this lace on your gown, so that you can have that same happiness. To know the love of a man who loves only you is the greatest gift of all."

Sarina hid the pang of sadness she felt at those words. Jason didn't love her. It was just sex to him. He had told her as much; she knew he was marrying her for his heir. The delicate antique lace from her mother's gown had been intricately sewn into the bodice of her gown.

The veil was attached to her head by the wedding tiara Jason's mother wore for her wedding. The tiara had a rich history as well. Jason's father, King Massimiliano, had presented the diamond circlet to his future queen at their engagement. Catarina wore that same tiara when she married Henri. The engagement ring that the king presented to his future queen, Rafaella, a square-cut emerald surrounded by diamonds, now belonged to Catarina, and she wore it always.

Jason, in full dress uniform as the Monarch of San Destino, was impressive, standing next to his best man, Henri. Catarina would walk with her two older children, Princess Simone and Prince Marcel, and the youngest, Princess Sara, would be in the arms of her godmother, Princess Carla, Jason's cousin. They were all in the wedding party.

The moment had arrived. Sarina put all thoughts of Jason never saying he loved her out of her mind. She loved him enough for the two of them. Unrequited love could work. He was marrying her because she was expecting his heir. Before that, he was sending her home at the end of the summer. He hadn't even asked her; he told her. She loved him and would make the marriage work. She hoped it would be enough.

She would be everything Jason wanted in a wife and queen. How would she live up to his mother and his sister? Catarina had been helpful and patient, guiding Sarina on royal protocol and her future duties.

Jason stood at the altar with Henri at his side, the cardinal in front. The wedding march was about to begin. The long aisle loomed before her, and Sarina for a panicked moment wondered if she could hear the music over the pounding of her heart.

She held on to her mother's arm. "Your father couldn't be

here for you," her mother said, "so I am happy to stand in and walk you to Jason."

"Royalty may walk alone. I read that somewhere, or maybe Catarina said it."

"You'll be royalty on the way down the aisle, but on the way up, you're still my baby."

She heard the emotion in her mother's voice.

Sarina's eyes welled up with tears. Patting her mother's hand, she said, "Please… Mom, don't… let me cry."

Her mother gave her a squeeze. They both took a deep breath at the same time the music began.

Royalty from around the world filled the seats, along with heads of state and dignitaries. There weren't too many relatives on Sarina's side; both her mother and father were only children. Some of her friends, the principal, and teachers from the school she had taught at, were there. The cathedral was decorated in beautiful pink and buttery yellow flowers, with sprigs of greenery held together with white satin ribbons. Tall candelabras were lit, and swags of fresh flower garland draped the altar. She held a small bouquet of gardenias and white roses tied with satin ribbon. Two memory charms were pinned to the ribbon, one of her father William Moore, and one of Jason's parents King Massimiliano and Queen Rafaella.

The ceremony, though an hour long, for Sarina flashed by before she could even register walking to Jason's side. She was on his arm now, and he led her out to the waiting carriage. An open-air, six-horse carriage waited at the steps of the cathedral.

The uniformed driver and footmen were in the colors of the Royal House of Donato, sapphire blue and gold. The carriage moved forward, taking them through the streets of San Destino's main piazza, on their way to the palace. The streets were lined with crowds of well-wishers cheering as the royal couple passed by.

"Smile and wave, my queen. Have I told you how beautiful you are?"

She shook her head.

"No?" he said. He smiled at her. "Well, you are the most beautiful woman I've ever known. If there weren't so many people—I would take you into my arms and do all sorts of wonderful things to make you moan in pleasure, *cara mia.*"

She melted at his words. Just a look or word, and she was ready for him. Would it always be like this? Once they were settled into married life, would he feel the same? Was it just the chase with him? Would he start up with his mistresses again? She didn't want to think of that, especially not today or any day, for that matter. Those weren't the best thoughts to have on her wedding day, her brain chided.

She smiled and waved to the crowds. She was floating on air when they reached the palace. The guests were waiting for the newlyweds. The bride and groom walked into the grand hall, taking their place in the receiving line. Sarina didn't know how she stayed on her feet all that time. Her silver and crystal shoes with their modest six-inch heels were pinching.

Lunch was served to the guests, while the traditional photos of the wedding party and family were taken in the throne room. The palace pastry chef had created a dream wedding cake, a magnificent, twelve-tier strawberry, vanilla custard, and yellow cake covered by a white fondant. Four footmen wheeled out the cake so that she and Jason could cut the first slice. Everything was wonderful, but Sarina leaned slightly on Jason's arm.

He turned and realized that it was a long day for her, and there was still more to come. He took Sarina to their rooms so she could rest before the wedding ball this evening. Sarina and Jason would have some time alone. He held her to him and kissed first one cheek, then the other, then placed his lips over hers and kissed her ever so gently. "How are you holding up?"

"I'm fine, Jason. It's just my feet are pinching." She hadn't suffered too much from morning sickness, and she had energy. Some days, in the middle of the afternoon, she would have to fight to keep her eyes open, but overall, the early stages of her pregnancy were going well. She wasn't even showing yet.

"Let me massage your feet."

"Mmmm oh?"

"We have time a few hours to ourselves… I made sure of that."

She giggled. "Do we really?"

He held her to him, and his lips found her warm mouth opening for him, inviting the slide of his tongue. She sighed before sucking on his tongue.

He held her to his body, moving his lips to her neck, nibbling the delicate skin. He breathed, "You have too many clothes on."

She gave him a throaty laugh that shot into his groin. "I don't even know where to begin or how to remove your uniform."

Now, it was his turn to laugh as he reached up and stripped out of his clothes.

Sarina watched him for a second before she turned and ran to the dressing room.

"I want to strip you," he'd said. The sight that greeted him made him stiff with arousal—

Her silk-covered derriere bent over, reaching to unbuckle the strap of her crystal-embellished shoe. She had placed her tiara, necklace, and earrings on a velvet tray on her dressing table. Her veil and wedding dress lay across the pink velvet divan on her side of the enormous room.

He sauntered over, taking her into his arms as he unhooked her bra, reaching both hands to her breasts, playing with the nipples, feeling them swell. His lips moved to the valley between, tracing a path to one pebble-hard nipple, his mouth replacing the hand that now slid over the satin skin of her waist to her back. "I missed you last night."

"I felt the same. I had fun talking with my mother and sister, but I missed you too."

It was time for the bride and groom to appear at the ball. Sarina had changed into another gown designed for her by a famous French designer. This one was ivory and off the shoulder, the skirt was satin, and on her head was another tiara, this one emeralds and diamonds. It came down and around her head more like a bandeau. Around her neck was a matching emerald-and-diamond necklace. The earrings she wore were the ones he had given her all those weeks ago. On her finger next to the engagement ring was the wedding band that Jason had surprised her with at the ceremony, an eternity band of diamond baguettes set vertically in platinum.

Jason and Sarina danced and laughed. Henri and Catarina made speeches, and so did Julia. Then it was time to leave. She kissed her mother, Julia, Catarina, and Henri goodbye.

Jason wanted to surprise her for their honeymoon, so he had one of the staff pack her bags. They drove down to the marina in his red Ferrari. As they approached, she saw the royal yacht all lit up, waiting for them. She yelped, "We're going on a cruise?"

He was taking her on a cruise of the Greek islands and the Amalfi Coast. Their first stop was a surprise.

The captain and the crew stood at attention, saluting as the newlyweds boarded. "Your Majesties, welcome aboard."

As the yacht left the dock, the night sky erupted with a firework display that lasted twenty minutes. They walked hand in hand to the master suite on the top deck of the yacht. When they reached the door, Jason turned the knob and pushed the door open. Before Sarina could take a step, he lifted her, carrying her over the threshold.

One wall of the bedroom was all windows overlooking the sea, the ceiling a glass dome. From the bed, all she could see was water. Lying on the bed, she could see the sky and the stars at night. It was amazing. She was hesitant at first, with all the windows, but Jason assured her that the glass was a one-way type where they could look out, but no one could see in. She laughed and said that she trusted him that they wouldn't be putting on a show for the crew with any of the activities they would have in their bed. He laughed and pulled her closer to him, then helped her out of her gown.

Their first stop was Palermo in Sicily. He wanted Sarina to share some of his mother's culture. Many of his mother's family, aunts, uncles, and cousins had been at the wedding. He drove Sarina up into the mountains to his ancestral home, and then they had lunch at one of his favorite restaurants. The food was delicious, and her choice of beverage was sparkling water. He told her that one day when they had more time, he would bring her back to Sicily so they could explore the island at their leisure.

They sailed on to Greece, exploring the many ruins, such as the Acropolis where the Parthenon and other ancient monuments were. At the ancient theater, they walked hand in hand as tourists. He told her that there was another in Sicily, and he would one day take her there.

On the yacht, they would lounge on deck, watch movies in the yacht's theater, and play chess in the game room. The chef went out of his way to make the best meals for them. On the way back to San Destino, they stopped in Sorrento. He told her the legend of how sirens tried to lure Odysseus onto the rocks. He took her to Capri, and they walked through the narrow streets, stopped at a restaurant for lunch, and then went back to the yacht. All too soon, it was over. She wished they could stay longer, but she knew Jason had to be back, so she said nothing, happy to have this time with him.

# CHAPTER 11

Once back from their honeymoon, Jason resumed his duties. Catarina and Henri had their children, their charities, and full schedules. Her mother and Julia had gone home, and Sarina was left with too much time on her hands. She read and relaxed and went for long walks in the private gardens of the palace. Growing bored and restless, she needed some activities.

One afternoon, Sarina found her way to Jason's office. She hadn't been there since that fateful day she was arrested, and his personal guard had brought her back from the airport.

The guards at his double doors clicked their heels and bowed their heads. "Your Majesty," they both said as they opened the white-and-gold ornate doors for her to enter.

Jason sat at his desk. Looking up, he smiled and motioned her in. His tie hung loose, the collar of his shirt unbuttoned, and his jacket hung over the back of his chair. He was on a conference call. He continued with the conversation, speaking French.

Her high school French was no match for him. She didn't

want to eavesdrop but couldn't keep up with what he was saying. When he finished and disconnected the call, he rose from his seat and came over to her, pulling her into his arms, kissing her.

The kiss started out gentle enough, but then his mouth slanted across hers, demanding a response. He kissed down the column of her neck as far as he could go before he reached fabric. Unzipping the back of her dress, he held her against his body, his erection pressing into her.

Her thoughts scattered as he slid the dress down her arms, no longer remembering why she had come to his office. She melted as he slid the dress down past her hips to pool at her feet, standing in her lacy bra and panties and high-heeled shoes.

"You make me so hot just looking at your beautiful body." He kissed her, stroking her tongue.

Heat radiated through Sarina. She held her breath as sensual heat flowed to her center, wanting more of what he offered. He brought her to the edge of his desk, lifted her, and she leaned back in his arms. Before she knew it, her bra came off.

His hot mouth found a breast, now more sensitive with the pregnancy. His teeth grazed her hard nipple, sending shivers of delight up her spine. Never leaving that breast, sucking the nipple, he cupped her other breast as his thumb stroked over the nipple.

She moaned, "Jason," as a zing of pleasure shot into her core. Her fingers worked frantically to unbutton his shirt.

He grinned and pulled the white silk shirt off in one motion. She unbuckled his black leather belt. He tugged her to him, planting kisses down her body, kissing her still-flat abdomen.

She wiggled on the edge of the desk, so hot for him. "Oh

yes. Please, please." She stretched her fingers to unzip his pants. "Please, Jason."

He stroked his hands down over her thighs to her knees, spreading her as he kissed her above the elastic of her sheer lace panties.

She groaned when he dropped to his knees. "Ohhh… Jason."

He slid the panties down and off her legs, then he leaned in, trapping her separated knees between his broad shoulders. "Lie back for me… I have to taste you."

Her core throbbed, and she bit back a moan, lying on the gleaming mahogany of his desk. He nuzzled the inside of her thigh, his hands holding her buttocks. He brushed a kiss at her center before his thumbs spread her open. His tongue licked her and sank into her core. She loved what he did, reaching his tongue deep into her. He sucked her inner folds before he rose. Shedding his shoes and pants, he said, "Put your legs around me, my beautiful wife."

She didn't hesitate as he lifted her up off the desk, walking with her wrapped around him to the sofa and sat, her knees on either side of his hips, straddling him. He played with her breasts, his fingers exciting the nipples.

Sarina held his face between her palms, kissing him, her fingers moving to the nape of his neck, her tongue darting around his. She pressed her breasts into his chest. Jason lifted her and slowly lowered Sarina onto him.

She gasped as inch by glorious inch, she sank onto his long, thick length. Each thrust went deeper and deeper. She was on fire. She couldn't do anything but hold onto him. His hands on her waist held her down, while his hips moved up with his powerful and deep thrusts. The deeper he went, the wilder she became, her body throbbing, her head thrown back, body arching, tempting him to suck a hard-pointed nipple into the heat of his mouth. When he did just that, she whimpered, holding his head to her.

A long, low moan erupted. Deep inside of her, the rolling waves radiated through her body as her orgasm clenched and unclenching around his steel-hard shaft. She couldn't get enough. He covered her mouth with his in an endless kiss. He caught first her moans and then scream in his mouth.

Sarina leaned forward against his strong chest, panting. She didn't want to let him go. He was rock hard in her. She moved her hips on him, and he held the globes of her buttocks in his hands. Sarina brought her lips to his, kissing him wildly, moving her hips the way he had taught her, lowering and rising herself. She wanted him to feel the way he always made her feel.

The exquisite tension drove her to the beginning of another orgasm. She needed the friction of his hard dick, and all at once, her climax stroked and clenched him as the waves of her orgasm took him deeper into her. She felt Jason shudder with his own release. She wanted to stay like this, wrapped in his arms forever.

"*Cara mia*, you have brightened my day with your beautiful body." He helped her back into her dress while he dressed. "I'm glad you came here today, *tesoro*. You'll have to visit me here more often." He smiled down at her, kissing her nose. "But then I'll never get any work done. What brought you here today?"

She looked at him, trying to remember. She had forgotten why she sought him out in the first place. Then she said, "I'm bored."

"Really? After this? I'll have to try harder." He took her hand. "Let's go." He started toward the door—

"No, Jason, I mean you have your work, Catarina and Henri have their children and charities, but I have nothing to do during the day. I need something to do while you're busy. I'll go crazy if I have nothing to keep me busy."

~

HE LOOKED DOWN AT HER, her lips kiss swollen, her hair wild with his fingers running through it. She was beautiful and would now be the mother of his children. What more than that? He understood. *I'd rather keep her naked and in our bed all day and night.* He knew she needed to occupy her time. "There are many charities that may interest you. You should start one or two of your own. You're a teacher. Perhaps you can take a tour of our schools, make some recommendations for improvements. I'll arrange for you to meet with the minister of education."

"I would also like to learn Italian. My high school French is poor, to say the least, and I would like to improve that." She smiled up at him. "I can speak Spanish… but I'm not fluent."

He put his arm around her shoulder and gave her a hug. "Come, I want to show you the adjoining office." He led her out a set of doors near his desk. They entered another office, smaller and decorated, like his. The desk wasn't as massive although made from the same mahogany wood.

The Persian area rug had lighter pinks and blues in the design, matching the drapes. A private patio could be accessed by the French doors directly behind the desk. Sarina ran a finger along the edge of the desk. She walked to the French doors and looked out onto the stone patio with two chaise lounges, a table, and chairs. Turning to Jason, she tilted her head, a frown on her face.

"This was my mother's. She wanted to be near my father, and so they had this room turned into her private office. It is now yours. I'll have a secretary and other staff hired for your personal use. I thought that you wanted some time to adjust to your new position. I should have realized sooner that you would need something to occupy your time. After all, you are not the type of person to just laze around. Forgive me?"

She reached up to touch his cheek. "Thank you for understanding." She frowned. "Why do I need a staff?"

"Someone to take care of your social calendar." He walked into his office and came back with a handful of envelopes that had been previously opened. "These are invitations and requests for appearances, yours and mine. Our social secretaries can organize which ones we agree to and help plan our day."

Sarina looked at the envelopes. She slipped out a card. "Oh, it's an invitation to a hospital opening." She took another. "And here is one to an opening of a new playground. This is wonderful."

"In the mix, there are invitations to socials, dinners, and a ball in Paris."

"Will you help me choose the ones you think I would like?"

He took the invitations, leaning his hip against the desk, his long fingers flipping through the stack, choosing what she might like to do. He looked up just as she tried to smother a yawn.

"You're tired. Is it the baby?" He moved away from the desk as she nodded. "Let me take you to our rooms." He left the invitations behind and led her down the corridor.

They strolled through the gardens holding hands, reaching their private residence. In the bedroom, Jason helped her out of her clothes. She put on a nightgown, and once in bed, he brushed a kiss on her lips, saying, "I'll wake you later… in a very special way."

Her eyelids slid closed, already drifting to sleep. She smiled. "Yes, please."

~

THEY BEGAN GOING OUT MORE, attending social events. Sometimes Catarina and Henri joined them. On one evening, at a ball in Paris, a tall, willowy blonde walked up to Jason. Sarina and Catarina were returning from freshening up and about to rejoin him. His back was to them, so he didn't see them approach. The woman looked at Sarina and Catarina.

She said hello to Jason, hugged his arm to her overflowing bosom, and leaned into him. "I am so happy to see you here, darling." She sneered in her heavy French accent. "Your wife has let you out... to have some fun?"

Sarina bristled, slowing her step.

"What have you been up to, Isobel?" Jason said in an impersonal tone.

"Oh, darling, you know... traveling, waiting for you to come to your senses. Will you dance with me?" He agreed and led her onto the dance floor.

Sarina stiffened. *The nerve of her.*

On the dance floor, Jason smiled at the blonde as he gave a slight bow. She stepped close to him. Her hips moved into his as her breasts pressed against his chest. From where Sarina stood, it looked as if he was certainly enjoying the close contact, more than his usual politeness.

Then, as Isobel swayed to the music, Sarina gasped. The woman's dress was sheer. She wore no lingerie of any kind, her buttocks visible. Jason spun her in the steps of the dance. Her breasts were clearly defined, the nipples rouged for all to see.

Sarina dared not look lower. The air felt heavy, and the room spun. Sarina knew the color had drained from her face.

Catarina saw the reaction and leaned closer to whisper. "Don't let him see you distressed."

"Who... is she?" Sarina managed in a tremulous voice.

"She's unhappy and stupid. Isobel expected to be queen. My father and hers were friends from childhood. I know my brother never gave her any encouragement. He was always courteous but never anything more. You know he believed women saw the title and the power, never the man." Catarina held Sarina's arm and, in a cheery voice, said, "Come, let's get a cold drink." Catarina and Sarina walked out of the ballroom.

The refreshments were in an adjoining room. Guests were milling about, the murmur of conversations all around, the music from the orchestra soft in the background. Waiters carried trays of crystal flutes filled with champagne for the guests.

Sarina walked to a waiter, requesting sparkling water. A wall of French doors was open, leading to a large terrace. The cool air was inviting. Catarina had gone in search of Henri, and Sarina walked slowly out onto the balcony. She didn't notice the lights of Paris. They were in the city of love, and she felt so alone.

Why did that woman make her feel insecure? Was it the venom she heard in her voice? Sarina could feel the woman's hatred. The way she danced with Jason, perhaps at one time they'd done more than dance. Could Isobel have been the lover he'd left in Paris? No, that wasn't her name. He'd said her name was Claudia, but surely, he'd had more than one mistress. Catarina said that Isobel and Jason weren't lovers... but maybe... she didn't know everyone Jason had been with.

Sarina stood at the edge of the terrace in the shadows when Jason came up to her. He slid his arm around her waist. "*Cara mia*, are you tired? Shall we go back to our suite?"

She leaned against his powerful, masculine body and laid her head back on his chest. "I am a little tired, but if you want to stay..." She was content in the circle of his arms, his handsome face in shadows, but his blue eyes made her blood heat.

He brushed a kiss on her temple. Sarina tilted her head up, looking into his eyes. She watched as a spark ignited in their depths.

"Let's go," he said. He intertwined his fingers with hers, and they walked out of the ball.

Jason and Sarina had decided that they would wait to announce the upcoming birth of their first child. Even with all his devotion to her, the nights and days filled with love-making, she was uncertain about Jason's feelings. He never said he loved her. He told her how beautiful she was and how grateful he was to have been the one who found her the night she ran away from the *Carmella*.

There were never any words of love. He called her *tesoro*, treasure, or *cara mia*, my darling. Sarina kept her words of love locked in her throat. At the palace after her arrest, when he'd brought her to his bedroom... he had said it was lust. That's all there was between them. She remembered those words; they haunted her. *Just sex, nothing more, never mistake this for love.*

Sarina thought she knew better, but he never said anything. She'd wanted him so much that she'd jumped at the chance to become his wife. She'd grabbed at it with both hands, willing to take crumbs to be with him. Now, well now, she didn't know what he thought. He never mentioned the baby, only to be sure that she was feeling well and not over-doing. He was always careful of her, never letting her do too much.

Each night, he would hold her in their bed, kiss her, caress her until she begged him to make her climax.

Sometimes, he would get in the shower or bath with her, making her wild as only he could. She loved the times they spent together... but lately, she wondered if he would grow tired of her and go in search of a new lover. Isobel wanted to star in that role. How would she handle that? Her thoughts tormented her, and she agonized over his taking another woman having sex with her.

Recently when they were in bed, after making love, for Sarina, that was what it was and always would be. The words of love caught in her throat, choking her. Jason would hold her in his arms, and she would cry.

The first time it had happened, he'd thrust one final time as they both climaxed. Panting heavily, he held her, kissing her temple. Her brain screamed, *I love you.* Her eyes were closed, and she felt him wipe a tear with his thumb. "Did I hurt you? You're crying—"

He sat up against the massive headboard, taking Sarina with him. "No. You didn't hurt me. It's just... actually..."

"Tell me why you're crying."

"Please—I can't. Hold me."

"Always, *cara mia.*"

OCTOBER CAME and went in a blur of activities. Jason and Sarina announced that Her Majesty Queen Sarina was expecting the next heir to the throne. Gifts for the baby poured in: handmade blankets, bibs, outfits, and stuffed animals. The people of San Destino were excited that the king and queen were expecting their first child, born sometime in late April.

The requests for Sarina to come to an opening or talk at a charity increased. They made several more appearances. In November, Sarina became melancholy. It wasn't like her to be depressed; she missed her mother and Julia. Surely that was all it was.

One night at dinner, she broached the subject of visiting her family. "I would like to go to Connecticut and see my mother and sister."

"What a good idea. Let me clear my calendar, and we can go at the end of next week."

She put her fork down. "I would like to go by myself. After all, you're busy. I can go alone."

Sarina watched the frown spread across his handsome face. She prepared to argue with him.

"Perhaps you need some time away from the demands of the palace. You'll still need security. As a member of the royal family, we'll have to take precautions for your safety," he said.

She looked across the table at him. "I'm going home, Jason… for a visit. To see my mother and sister, not anything else. I'll be all right."

He shook his head. "It's settled. You'll have your security team from the royal guard accompany you."

There it was again, the king's decree. "Well, if you insist, but one minor question, Jason. Where in my mother's tiny two-bedroom apartment will they sleep?"

He laughed at that but said nothing else.

That night, for the first time, all he did was pull her into his arms and hold her, nothing more.

She felt worse. Hiding her tears from him, she fell asleep. In the morning, he held her and kissed the nape of her neck and her shoulder. She felt him hard against her buttocks. She needed him as much as he wanted her, pressing back against his body. Jason slid a hand down over the slight rounding of her abdomen.

A MOVEMENT against his palm brought his head up in surprise. Leaning over her, he asked, "Did the baby kick?"

"I think so. It's the first time that I've felt anything like that!"

He brushed a kiss on her shoulder, sliding his hand over her abdomen.

Another movement, and Sarina smiled up at him. "It feels so funny and wonderful at the same time."

He caressed her lips with feather-light sweeps of his until she leaned back against his chest, cradled in his arms, with their baby moving in her. He bent over and kissed her belly. Jason held her to his chest, and the kicks stopped.

Sarina covered his hand with hers before nudging it to her breast.

"Are you sure?" he said.

"Of course." She smiled up at him, pressing his hand to her.

He plucked at the nipple, nipping at her neck, sliding his hand down from her breast, over her abdomen, over her mound. He rubbed his open palm on her. She parted her legs, encouraging him. One finger traced her seam, dipping in; he rubbed her clit.

"Ahh. Jason."

He traced her folds tenderly and slowly before slipping his finger into her core.

Sarina turned her head, offering her lips to him. He slowly descended to cover her mouth, kissing her. One hand on her breast, exciting the peak, his finger loving her below, his tongue in her mouth, mimicking the slide of his finger, his erection pressing against her buttocks. She had his baby growing in her; she was surrounded by him and never wanted this to stop.

Thoughts of other women fled her mind. Her hips bucked, and she gasped at the exquisite pleasure, lifting her leg over his hip, opening herself to him. She moaned as she felt another finger slide into her; she was burning up.

He moved his fingers, reaching into her.

She whimpered against his mouth. His lips muffled her moans.

"You are wild in your pleasure. I want to feel you come like this." He breathed against her mouth.

She moaned, and all he needed to do was apply a very slight pressure to her clit. She screamed into his mouth, her hand holding his to her as her hips bucked. "Yes, Jason, I want…"

~

Sarina lay still in his arms. As her breath returned to normal, he gently replaced his fingers with his throbbing length, small thrusts until he was buried deep in her.

She moaned, "Oh yes."

He held her leg over his hip and kept the thrusts smooth and shallow.

Sarina was too hot and wild to just lay there. She moved her hips back to meet his thrusts, taking him deeper. He wasn't sure how much longer he could hold back. He wanted her to climax again and again. When he felt the beginning of her orgasm, he stopped thrusting. She groaned, "Please, please."

Her muscles tighten around him. He thrust deeply, once, twice, three times, and she exploded around him. He wanted her to always remember him, to never forget the pleasure he gave her. When she calmed, he rolled her onto her back; he was still hard.

He kissed her breasts and licked her nipples before moving down her body. *I have to taste her.* Lowering his head, his tongue touched her clit, circling the bud, lashing at her wet folds, dipping into her vagina. *Ahh, so good, my sweet beauty.* Hot honey greeted him as he branded her with his special kind of sex. He would make her remember him, always.

She moaned, a long, low sound as she held his head. Her fingers twisted in his hair, and her hips rose, wanting his tongue to go deeper. She was wild as he spread her wider, his tongue licking all of her before he thrust it into her hot center. She whimpered, calling out his name as she climaxed.

He lifted himself before her last spasm stopped and entered the hot volcano that was Sarina. "Look at me."

She opened her eyes. The emerald green blazed with desire.

"You're mine. Always. Mine."

"Yes, Jason, always."

He wanted her to remember what he did to her and how much she needed him. Only him.

"Jason… love me, please."

"Every day and night."

This time, she didn't cry. She fell asleep almost before he finished pouring himself into her. It was mid-morning when Sarina woke up, wrapped in Jason's arms. He'd held her while she slept.

# CHAPTER 12

$S$arina had gone home five days ago. In that time, Jason realized how big and empty the palace felt. That was a new sensation. *I am lonely for her... I miss her.* He'd never experienced that before. His duty had almost become a burden.

Never did he need anyone to come home to talk with, share his day. *When did she become such a part of my life, needing her for my very existence?*

They spoke every day on the phone; she sounded tired, but with the time difference, it was understandable.

The royal jet was landing, and Jason had gone to the airport to meet Sarina. Jason held an enormous bouquet of gardenias ready to present to her. A band waited along with a large contingent of children and adults. The door of the royal jet opened. She came forward wearing a dress of deep royal blue silk brocade with a matching coat, her fiery locks piled up in a twist, the sunlight turning it red gold. Sarina wore black high-heeled shoes.

She scanned the crowd, saw him, and smiled. Then she waved to the throng of people and proceeded down the steps onto the red carpet. Jason came forward, gave her the flowers, and kissed her on one cheek, then the other. Sarina greeted the ministers and other people who came to welcome her home. Jason took her arm and led Sarina to the waiting car. He helped her in and slid in beside her. The car drove off toward the palace; the streets were lined with people. She waved to them and offered a brilliant smile.

"You were missed," he said, his thumb rubbing her fingers.

She turned to him. "As were you. I'm happy to be home."

She needed to see her mother and sister, but the surprise that awaited her when she arrived in Connecticut was wonderful. Jason, always so generous and saying nothing to her, had bought her mother a house. Her heart warmed, thinking of him and his all-encompassing generosity.

Julia wouldn't have to worry about working and could concentrate fully on her studies. Jason paid for her schooling. He'd told Julia that he hoped when she became a doctor, she would practice medicine in San Destino. He wanted Sarina's mother to live on the island. Jason wanted his children to have a grandparent in their lives.

Sarina knew when they married, Jason would provide for her family. Jason had said, "You are not to concern yourself. *Cara mia*, your family will be taken care of. I have my own wealth, and what better use than to provide for your family? After all, they'll be my family as well, grandmother and aunt to our child. You do not have to worry." She didn't know the extent, though she should have guessed. Her mother and Julia would spend Christmas with them at the palace.

His deep voice interrupted her thoughts. "You look well. How do you feel?"

"I'm happy I could visit with my mother and sister but so very, very glad to be home." Sarina held his hand.

"I hope you're in the mood to see Catarina and Henri. They've invited us to their apartment for dinner."

Though she was tired, she smiled. "Yes, that will be nice. I want to see them too."

Jason noticed that she looked much better than she had sounded on the phone. When they arrived at their apartment, Sarina kicked off her shoes, dropped her coat to the floor—not her usual way—and turned her back to him. "Please, unzip me. I have to have a bath."

As he pulled the zipper down, he said, "I'll go fill the tub."

"I'm so tired. Do you think I'll have time for a nap before we have to go?"

"Yes, you do. We can cancel if you wish."

"Oh no, Jason, it'll be good to see them and the children. After dinner, you and I can relax here at home."

He kissed her lightly on the lips and left her to her bath. He waited until she was done, then he tucked her into bed. "You sleep. I'm going to the office for a while. I'll wake you later."

She smiled at him. "I hope in a very special way," she said and drifted off to sleep.

THE HOLIDAYS BROUGHT many more party invitations. Isobel was always present. She wore the most revealing gowns, though none as daring as the see-through one she wore in Paris. The countess was always on the arm of a different man. They all seemed to be much older than she.

Sarina never brought up the fact that she had heard Isobel or the dance she and Jason shared. At one such party, Sarina had walked out onto the balcony for a breath of air. She saw Jason and Isobel in the shadows; they didn't see her, and she was about to turn away when she heard his voice. "You will show respect to my wife, your queen. I'll tolerate none of your petty animosity toward her. Thoughts of a marriage between us were solely in your head. I never led you to believe otherwise. There never was more between us."

"You wanted me. I know you did."

"When you gyrated your hips against me, I was repulsed." His barely suppressed anger coming through his voice, he said, "Never dance with me in such a manner again. Go cover yourself!"

IT WAS NOW A NEW YEAR. Sarina blossomed, and the pregnancy agreed with her. They spent many a pleasant hour in bed, Jason always careful of the baby. The doctor had assured Sarina that she could continue all her activities, just rest as much as possible. She and Jason were making plans for the baby. She thought that the nursery was too far from their rooms. One night, while they were relaxing on the terrace, she brought up the subject. "I would like the baby closer to us."

Jason wasn't surprised. Though he had never thought about it, the nursery was in another wing of the palace. "We can turn the rooms on the other side of the sitting room into a nice nursery suite. We can even have a place for a nanny."

"Oh yes, that would be wonderful."

He kissed her temple. "Tomorrow, we'll call a decorator and get started. After all, we only have three months."

The time flew by, and the nursery was ready. She and Jason didn't want to know if it was a prince or a princess she carried, so they decorated the nursery in mint green and yellow.

Sarina's mother had flown in and would stay several months. With the green light from Sarina's doctor, Jason made plans to take the two of them to London for some baby shopping. In the evening, he took them to the theater. Julia wouldn't be there when the baby was born, but once her classes finished, she would spend the summer with them. She planned on taking some online courses, so she could be near Sarina and the baby.

One morning a few days later, Sarina woke up with a start, a heavy, uncomfortable feeling spreading through her abdomen. *Could this be labor?*

Jason, his arms around her, asked, "What is it? Is it the baby?"

"I think so."

He sat up. "I'll call the doctor."

"No, Jason, we have time. I'm in the early stages if it even is labor." Sarina got out of bed. As she walked to the bathing suite, her water broke. "Oh." She stood there for a moment, a look of surprise on her beautiful face. "I think I just wet myself. Ouch… ohh."

"Now will you let me call the doctor?" he asked, the phone already in his hand.

"Yes, call!"

The doctor met them at the entrance to the hospital with a wheelchair. In the end, Sarina needed to have a c-section. The handsome baby boy weighed nine pounds. And from his length, he would be as tall as his father.

Sarina was in a private suite at the hospital. There were two large beds in the room she occupied; a sofa and two wing chairs faced the beds, and the nursery adjoined with an additional sleeping area for the nurse. Sarina lay asleep in one bed, an IV in one arm. Recovering from the anesthesia, she had become restless.

Jason was reclining in an oversize chair next to her bed when he heard her mumble, "He doesn't love me. It was only sex. Lust, he said…" She tossed her head. "I love him so much. I love him."

He looked at her in surprise. She finally quieted down and fell into a deeper sleep. Jason sat there, staring at her. She loved him. Love? What was love? He loved his country, his family. He cared deeply for Sarina. His sexual desire for her knew no boundaries. But love. That was for other people. He was above the emotion; he had responsibilities that didn't include love.

Jason stood and paced the room. Turning, his eyes became two slits as he stared at her. She slept so peacefully, her bright-red hair spread out around her angel's face. Did he overlook something? He cared deeply for Sarina. In bed, sex with her was never better. He never reached the level of intensity with anyone else ever. He wanted to protect her and keep her safe, especially from women like Isobel and men like Chad. He wanted to make her happy. Was that love? She brightened his day. A smile spread across his lips.

With his other mistresses, once he was finished, he couldn't wait to get out of bed. He may have briefly held them in his arms after sex, but it was always uncomfortable. It wasn't so with Sarina. He had to hold her, touch her; his mind and body demanded it.

The doctor came in. "Your Majesty, the queen is doing well and should sleep through the night, and the young prince, your son, is in the adjoining room. Would you care to hold him? If you wish, I'll stay with Her Majesty."

"Thank you, Doctor."

The nurses were sitting by the bassinet when Jason walked in. They stood and curtsied. "Your Majesty."

He went to the bassinet and looked down at his sleeping son. One nurse came over. "Your Majesty, would you care to hold your son?"

He nodded. "Yes."

The nurse picked up the baby and placed him in his father's arms.

The emotions going through him were amazing, and none he'd ever experienced before. Naturally pride, but this little baby conceived in a blind moment of lust, when he forgot to use a condom, touched a place in his heart that he didn't realize was there.

Love for a child, so powerful. He looked down at his son and thought of his parents. How they always made time to spend with him and Catarina. The way Catarina and Henri are with their children. Parenthood, love. This was something he needed to delve into more deeply.

He thanked the nurses and gently lay his son back in the bassinet and went to Sarina.

"Thank you, Doctor. I'll spend the night here."

She rested quietly. There was no more talking in her sleep. Jason heard her move and sat up. "Good morning, *tesoro*. Would you like to see our son?"

Her smile brightened the room. "Yes, yes, yes."

He had the nurse bring in the sleeping infant.

SARINA HELD him for the first time. He had a full head of hair the same color as his father and eyelashes girls would die for. He moved and opened his eyes; they were blue! But all babies had blue eyes, didn't they?

"Oh, look! Hello, my darling. I'm your mommy, and I love you very much. Jason, he is so handsome, not red and scrunched up."

He smiled at her. "Yes, that seems to be the consensus. Your mother, Catarina, and Henri were here last night to see him, and they felt the same way."

"Oh, look, he's cooing at us."

They had already decided on a name for the new prince

and future king. He would be known as Alberto William Massimiliano Stefano of the House of Donato—William, after her father, Massimiliano, after Jason's father, and Stefano, after the first king of San Destino. Over one thousand years of kings and queens from this family. The pride Jason felt was immeasurable.

~

SARINA AND JASON were back at the palace for well over six weeks. They shared their bed, but it was too soon to resume any intimate relations. He held her in his arms each night. She was happy to be there and hopeful that at her next visit, the doctor would tell her she could resume all activities. She seemed to be recovering well from the c-section.

Sarina took almost exclusive care of the baby. Jason and Sarina shared the night feedings. If need be, her mother was nearby as well. Sarina bathed her son in the mornings, and Jason usually stayed nearby. She changed the baby, fed him, and took him for walks in his carriage. Sarina could usually be found with the baby on the terrace adjoining their bedroom.

The weather was warm, so she would have the carriage brought down to the gardens and take the baby for walks there. Her mother and Julia would join her, and they would have lunch together. Some days, Catarina and her three children would join her. They would all have lunch on the patio by the pool. The older children played in the pool while the little one toddled around with her nanny following. The baby, in his carriage, slept in the shade. Sarina was never far from him.

When Alberto was two months old, he was christened. Sarina wore a dress that showed the world that she had regained her figure. That day, Jason, with Sarina holding the baby, made the traditional appearance on the balcony of the palace. The gates had been opened to allow well-wishers into the inner courtyard to see the royal family. The crowds cheered. All that was missing was Jason's love for her. She thought perhaps one day that would come.

Soon after the christening, Sarina decided to take matters into her own hand. She had a special dinner prepared for her and Jason to be served out on their private terrace off the master bedroom. The night was warm, the air scented from the gardens below. It was a little over one year from that night when he found her on the side of the road. She was wearing the green dress he had given her all those months ago. On her feet were sexy, gold, high-heeled sandals. She wore her favorite emerald earrings and pendant, the ones Jason had given her. Her only other jewelry was her engagement ring and wedding band; those she never took off her finger. Her red hair was loosely piled in a messy bun on her head, with wisps of auburn curls escaping at her temples and her neck.

She turned and saw him, and her breath caught in her throat. Her husband, so handsome, tall, broad shoulders, narrow hips, the power that lay under his suit. All at once, she felt shy.

He came over to her and kissed her on the temple. "Hello, my heart. What a pleasant surprise, dinner out here. How is our son?"

"He's doing well. The doctor said he was at the top of his percentile, growing and thriving. We both had our doctor visits today."

"Yes?" Jason perked up, his arm around her waist, looking

down into her emerald-green eyes. "How is everything with you?"

"My doctor said I'm in perfect health and can resume all my activities whenever I want."

"Well, that's wonderful news." He poured them both a glass of champagne. He raised his glass. "Here's to the most beautiful woman I know. You're my wife, my lover, my queen, and the mother of my child." They touched glasses and sipped the bubbly liquid. He pulled out a chair for Sarina to sit, and then he took his seat across from her.

The servants brought out the meal. Sarina and Jason talked about the day and their upcoming visit to the United Nations. They would both be meeting with dignitaries from other countries to discuss commerce in San Destino. She didn't want to leave Alberto, so arrangements had to be made to bring a large contingent of the royal household with them. This would prepare them for later in the year when they went to Australia on tour.

They talked about the baby, laughed, and enjoyed their meal. He poured them both an after-dinner brandy and dismissed the servants. Alberto was with his nanny for the night. Jason and Sarina, hand in hand, strolled through the gardens, the air heavy with jasmine and gardenia as they walked back to their rooms.

He took her in his arms. Her kisses were always electrifying. He stroked her tongue with his, pulling her seductive form closer to his body. He had been thinking of this moment since she said that she could resume all her activities. His erection had swelled, and now his fingers found the zipper of her dress. He kissed down her neck as the dress pooled around her feet. She reached for the buttons of his shirt.

"No, all for you, my heart," he said, brushing her hands to her sides. Stepping back, he looked at her. Her body had become more desirable if that were possible. Jason had counted the weeks as they turned into two months. He wasn't sure if he could wait to be in her again.

Jason unclasped her bra. Her breasts were bigger and still firm. He cupped each one, then he bent his head and circled the tight nipple of one breast with his tongue, sucking it into his mouth, then the other. He was determined to go through with this. Jason slid her panties down her legs and lifted one sandaled foot, and she moved her hands to his shoulders. Naked now, leaving on the gold stiletto sandals and her jewelry. Her hair had come loose when his fingers pulled the pins out, dropping them to the floor as her silken curls tumbled around her shoulders.

On his knees, he nudged her legs apart, sliding his hands up her ankles, past the curve of her calves, up the backs of her thighs, over her buttocks, one round globe in each of his hands. He pressed her close to his mouth, closer, as his tongue snaked out. He heard Sarina moan even before he spread her.

She held onto his shoulders. His tongue finding her hidden bud, loving her. He pulled her close.

She called his name on a sigh. "Jason."

He felt her juices flow like lava. His tongue went around her bud and into her center, and her core throbbed.

"Oooh, Jason, oh, Jason, yes, yes, please."

He heard the wild need in her pleas. *I miss her abandon.* He held one leg and guided it to his shoulder. A long moan escaped her, his hands back, holding her buttocks. Pulling her closer to his mouth, he tasted the hot honey that was Sarina. Her fingers tangled in his hair. He felt her spasms begin as he pushed his tongue into her center, and she climaxed.

It was wonderful for him; he wanted to give her more of the sweet pleasure. Now he knew he had always loved her.

Sarina's leg relaxed, and he raised himself, scooping her into his arms and carrying her to the bed. He gently placed her in the middle of the bed, his mouth covered hers in a hungry kiss.

He tore off his shirt, and the rest of his clothes followed. Naked, he came to her. She gazed up at him. The love he saw in the emerald depths almost broke him. "I have to be in you. Now. I can't wait any longer."

"Yes, yes, I need you too."

He came over her, and she spread her legs, reaching to guide him. He entered her as he kissed her sweet mouth. She was wild for him. He couldn't get deep enough. He lifted her legs over his shoulders, and she encouraged him to go deeper and deeper, thrust after marvelous thrust, tossing her head from side to side. He could feel her climaxing again. "Look at me," he said. She opened her eyes. They were passion glazed.

"I love you, Sarina," he breathed in a hoarse whisper. The hot, sweet liquid surrounded him. Buried deep in her again, he said, "I love you, little thief. You've stolen my heart."

She held him tighter. "I love you so much, Jason." He climaxed.

When their breathing returned to normal, Sarina turned in his arms. She kissed him, and he gave her a squeeze.

He moved to her side, holding her in his arms. "In the hospital after Alberto was born, you were talking in your sleep. You said that I had said we only had sex. The day I said that to you, I was angry because you wanted to leave me. Never angry about the jewels, only that you wanted to leave me." He stroked her flushed cheek. She looked up at him.

His blue eyes beseeching her, he said, "I'm sorry about that. I've always loved you, though I didn't know it at the beginning." He smiled at her. "I've been yours since the moment we met. You'll never have cause to doubt my love, ever." He pulled her to him. "I love you, Sarina."

****

Thank you for reading A ROYAL TEMPTATION I hope you enjoyed Sarina and Jason's story. I will have more royal love stories soon.

Have you read The Sicilian's Betrayal? It's the first book in the DiMarco Empire Series.

Forced to marry the Sicilian billionaire....

Elizabeth Ferguson believes that Ricardo DiMarco does not want the child she carried....years later a chance encounter brings Liz face to face with the brooding Sicilian billionaire. He can never know she kept the child he didn't want.

Ricardo DiMarco has always lusted for the luscious green eyed siren who left him to marry another man. Discovering her single and working in a jewelry store, he plans a tantalizing revenge. Getting Liz fired and seducing her with his expert touch is only the beginning. He won't allow her to slip through his fingers this time.

Grab this first book in the DiMarco Enterprises Series
The Sicilian's Betrayal

# ALSO BY CINDY REDDING

*The DiMarco Empire Series*

The Sicilian's Betrayal

The Winemaker's Seduction

The Frenchman's Revenge

The Sea Captain's Redemption

**Christmas**

A Fake Date for Kate

**The Royals**

A Royal Temptation

**More Romances**

The Tycoon's Secret Child

# WHERE TO FIND MY BOOKS

*You can find my books at your favorite bookstore, retailer, or library* 

*Or, you can buy them directly from me at my website https:// CindyReddingAuthor.com*

*Or,*

*Cindy's Store https://payhip.com/CindyRedding*

*If you prefer, please scan this QR Code with your phone*

# ABOUT THE AUTHOR

USA TODAY Bestselling Author **Cindy Redding** fell in love with happily ever after when she read her first romance at age twelve. Since then, she has been hooked.

A native New Yorker, Cindy lived on the beach in South Florida and now she lives in Las Vegas, NV, with her husband, of thirty-five years whom she married on Valentine's Day. She has two daughters. Her eldest is named after a heroine in one of Cindy's favorite romances.

Inspired by her travels around the world and her love of Italy Cindy's, sizzling contemporary romance novels come to life with hot men and the strong-willed, independent women who can tame them.

Escape into a world were happily ever after, lives.

When she's not writing, you can find her taking long walks in the desert or driving to Disneyland.

# ACKNOWLEDGMENTS

I want to thank Heather Starling for her invaluable advice.
    I would like to thank SJS Editorial Services for their thorough editing.

9 7 9 8 9 8 5 9 9 1 9 0 1